Covering her ASSETS

Dix Dodd Mysteries

The Case of the Flashing Fashion Queen (#1)
Family Jewels (#2)
Death by Cuddle Club (#3)
A Moment on the Lips (a Dix Dodd short story)

Check out Dix Dodd's website:
http://www.dixdodd.com

A Dix Dodd Mystery

N.L. Wilson

(The writing team of Norah Wilson and Heather Doherty)

PUBLISHED BY:

Something Shiny Press
P.O. Box 30046, Fredericton, NB, E3B 0H8

Edited by Jeni Chappelle
Proofread by Yolande Gagnon
Book Cover by The Killion Group Inc.
Formatted by IRONHORSE Formatting

ISBN: 1927651166
ISBN-13: 9781927651162

CHAPTER 1

LIFE'S FUNNY.

Okay, not always in that *ha ha, the-dirtbag-ex-boyfriend-fell-down-a-well* funny. Yet while I'm thinking of it, ha ha, my dirtbag ex-boyfriend fell down a well. But that's neither here nor there. What I'm saying is that life can be...*weird* funny.

Yeah, weird funny. Let's go with that. And why not? That about sums up the last few months of my life.

Business has been great. No complaints there. Lots of down-and-dirty in Marport City to keep this private detective very happy. And yeah, a big chunk of my business was still who's cheating on whom. Not to mention *with* whom. Also, where, when, how, and even for how long. And some of them were pretty long, in my learned experience...and I do research.

Oh, the snapshots I was getting of sneaking-around spouses. Some of them were downright giggle-worthy.

It wasn't just cheating spouses that kept my camera clicking. Increasingly, other business was coming our way. Well, trickling in.

Yes siree, the Dodd-Foreman partnership was working out nicely. That's right—no more apprentice work for Dylan. We were business equals on paper and in every other way. Though, I sometimes had a hard time wrapping my head around it. Admittedly, I did have a wee bit of trouble *letting go* with Dylan. But I was trying.

Since that crazy case of Death by Cuddle Club, we'd even picked up a couple of stalk-the-stalker cases. Gotta love referrals. Stalker cases are similar to pin the tail on the donkey, except I pin the incriminating pics on the asses who were supposed to be staying well away from their former lady loves. (Hello peace bond, anyone?) Intense cases, those ones.

We had a couple of nice missing person cases too. Nice because we found the missing persons—easily solved by yours truly. Fortunately, they were all thrilled to have been looked for, let alone found.

Then there was that whole thing with Tatum Banks. Rochelle so owed me on that one! And everyone saw this debt except Rochelle. She still wouldn't pay up. Paying up being dishing the dirt on her new flame, Detective Richard Head. Was that so much to ask?

Okay so I knew who and with whom in this case. But what about the rest of it? How was the sex? You know the whole...where? when? how long? How long, as in how long they'd been seeing each other. Geez, get your mind out of the gutter! Only 'cause it's getting crowded and I was here first. (First...perpetually...I get those two mixed up.)

Again, was that so much to ask? It's just normal girl talk, right? But Rochelle wouldn't even be goaded into it.

Just so we're clear, Rochelle wasn't the only one getting some action.

Let me rephrase that:

ROCHELLE WASN'T THE ONLY ONE GETTING SOME ACTION!

That's right—I'm shouting. I actually have a love life! Like, with a real person and everything.

And not just any real person. With a hot one. One of those yummy manly men.

Since the Cuddle Club case—yes, I still have nightmares about that whole cuddle experience—Dylan Foreman and I have been a couple.

Actually, it had been exactly three months. Kind of cool.

My mother, Katt Dodd, was over-the-top thrilled. Mrs. Jane Presley? Well, she knew all along that we'd end up together. And me? I was happy. Cautiously happy. And yeah, scared to death, doing this relationship thing.

I know. Hard to believe, tough-as-nails Dix Dodd doing *close*. And yes, we were also doing *it* too—just ask Rochelle. Oh dear God, no, she wasn't watching! See, I gave up the details. Lots and lots of details. Too many? Yeah, like there's such a thing between BFFs.

Perhaps I wasn't doing close-close, but I was getting closer to it.

The fact is, I have a boyfriend. Wow, that still blows my mind.

So why the lament that life is weird? Because, like with everything else in my world, this traditional relationship couldn't be smooth going...

Or maybe I couldn't let it be.

That sounds like me.

Dylan Foreman is twenty-nine. Go ahead, do the math. At pushing forty-one, I'm well within that half-your-age-plus nine range—it *is* nine, right? Dylan's great. He's one of the good guys.

Oh, but that down-the-well boyfriend scenario I referenced earlier? There's a reason that brings a smile to my face. A bitter one.

Yup. I've had my own share of heartache. A big slice of it named Myles Gauthier.

Suffice it to say, I swore I'd never let my guard down or love that much again. After I kicked Myles to the curb, I swore I would never again let anyone get close. One of those nobody's-that-rich-or-that-well-hung vows.

Well, Dylan's not rich...

The point being, despite my past crappy experiences with Myles—yes, *experiences* plural; I'm a slow learner sometimes—I was trying with Dylan. It was new for him too. Dating the former-boss-turned-business-partner. Sleeping with an older woman. An *amazing* older woman. And though he was always very guarded, very mum, on the subject, I knew Dylan had once had his heart broken too. But not as bad as mine, I'd bet.

Except he wouldn't bet.

Which told me there was still a sting there.

Truly, there are no two people on the planet more competitive than me and Dylan. You'd think our romantic involvement would have lessened that. You'd be thinking wrong. It only intensified it.

Take our one month anniversary, for example. I hadn't even realized we had been dating one whole month when the fourteenth of December rolled around. But Dylan, the romantic, brought me a heart-shaped cookie that morning, still warm from Perky Joe's coffee shop around the corner. Dylan had obviously unwrapped the plastic and microwaved it there; nothing's fresh from the oven at Perky Joe's. Sweet? Yes, even I know cookies are sweet. Quite often chocolaty too.

It was a thoughtful gesture. Under normal circumstances, this would be kind of cute. But these weren't normal circumstances—this was Dylan and me.

"Didn't you remember our anniversary, Dix?" he'd asked. He'd had that smarmy smile on his face. That one-up smile.

I hadn't, of course.

"Of course I remembered!" I said. "I...I have a little something for you right...where did I put it?" I started rummaging through the things on my desk to find something—anything—resembling a gift. But somehow a length of staples and ball of rubber bands just didn't say *oh baby, oh baby*. I did have a rubber thimble with little nubby bumps all over it… Of course, that would be more for me than him. The things he could do with those nubby bumps...

Dylan had known I was bluffing about having a gift for him. He used that to his advantage.

Well played, Mr. Foreman...well played.

"It's okay, Dix. Just because our relationship means so much to me doesn't mean it has to be the same for you." He kissed me on the forehead and went back to his office, where he snagged the mailbox key and headed out the door.

The prick! That meant war!

Before I even took a single bite of that cookie, I threw on my coat, grabbed my purse, and raced across the office to the door. Then—what was I thinking?—I dashed back to that cookie.

With a mouthful of chocolate chip, I zoomed over to the pharmacy not far from the office. It was a block away, right next to Stoner Stan's, the adults-only toy, video, and smoke shop.

"Hi ya, Dix," Stan called to me as I ran past. "How's your mom? I haven't seen her in ages."

I didn't have time to chat. Much. "Katt's great, thanks Stan. Oh, and I'll pick up my order on Wednesday! Say hi to Bambi and the kids. Talk soon!"

He waved me along. As I took off again, I almost ran down a little old lady. If she hadn't jumped her pink- and blue-haired self out of the way, we'd have collided.

"Watch it, Dixie-Doodle."

What? Was that a lucky guess? She did look vaguely familiar…

But the clock was ticking. I didn't have time to ponder where I might have seen her before. So I carried on, blasted through the pharmacy door, and slid around the corner to the greeting card aisle. I just needed to get one of those sappy cards, sign it, and have it on Dylan's desk before he returned with the mail. I snatched up the first romantic-looking card I could find. There was a loving duo on the front. Great! I glanced inside and didn't see the words *DEEPEST SYMPATHY*. Perfect.

I practically threw the money across the counter at the clerk, pulled a pen from my purse, and scribbled a little something on the inside of the card.

I shoved the card into the envelope and then plowed through—er, passed by—that tough-looking pair of Salvation Army folk in front of Perky Joe's.

I tossed the card onto Dylan's desk and dove back in behind mine a full two seconds before he came back into the office.

"Happy..." *Puff puff...need air now.* "One month..." *Stitch in side...killing me.* "Anniversary!"

Dylan smiled as he picked up the card. Then he opened it and looked absolutely stricken. Pale as a sheet. Scared shitless.

"What?" I panted. "What's wrong?"

Big, tall, strapping Dylan Foreman didn't scare easily, but as he read the card again—out loud that time—he looked petrified. "*Congratulations on your pregnancy*?" He looked up at me. "Dix are you...are we…? I mean, I thought you'd put a little weight on, but—"

"No!" I protested. "You've got it all wrong… I retain water! It's a hormone thing."

"But...but you inscribed the card. 'To Dylan, from Dix...may there be many more.' Wait a minute…" His voice went comically high. His eyes shot to my stomach. "How many have you got in there?"

"It was a mistake, okay?"

"We sure as hell didn't plan it."

"Whoa! Dylan, take it easy," I said. "There's nothing in this oven. I must have picked up the wrong card."

He started to get it, as evidenced by the color that was coming back into his cheeks.

"Wait a minute." His eyes narrowed on me. "Don't tell me you just ran to the pharmacy while I was getting the mail and grabbed the first card you came to that had a couple on it. Surely you're not that competitive, Dix."

I said nothing. He had, after all, told me not to tell him.

But that was the only time he'd managed to one-up me on an anniversary.

At the two month mark, I came into the office first thing in the morning to find him leaning on my desk, a dozen roses in hand. But I'd been ready. Well prepared and planning for days. That's right: I gave him the rubber thimble after all. 'Cause the more I thought about nubby bumps…

That was a month ago.

So there we were, three months down the line. To the day. February fourteenth. I'd circled it in red on the calendar so I'd remember. Too anxious to sit, I stood leaning against my desk in the bright and early morning, sipping my coffee, and I knew I had that I'm-so-smart smile on my face. I know 'cause I kept checking it in the mirror. I watched the clock. And I watched the door.

I knew Dylan would soon arrive. But I had no idea who else would be charging/sashaying through our office door that day.

Did I mention how weird my life is?

It was just about to get weirder.

"Happy three months!" Dylan was calling the words out even as he opened the door. I mean, his hand was literally still gripping the door knob. Only one size thirteen foot was over the office threshold. No, I hadn't heard him approaching—I'll give him that. He'd sneaked up to the door as quietly as he could and surprised me with his entrance.

Romantic on his part?

Not a chance. He wanted to catch me giftless yet again. With no chance of saving face by running out for a card. And he knew I'd not been to Staples in weeks, so I couldn't even offer up a shapely pencil nub from my desktop. He wanted to catch me with that crap-I-forgot look on my face.

Told you it meant war.

In your face, Foreman!

He only got a very smug smile from me as I set my coffee down and picked up the wrapped gift from my desk. That's correct: wrapped. Ribbons and a bow.

His eyes lit up. "Well, good morning."

He locked the door behind him and strode into the office purposefully. No one would be barging in on us. There was a decisiveness to that flip of the deadbolt, not to mention the way Dylan shrugged out of his winter coat.

He crossed toward me at a leisurely, confident pace. He nodded a quick hello to Blow-up Betty sprawled out on the sofa. Then those chocolate brown eyes were back on me, raking their way down my body.

I went from zero to horny with every step he took. And when he arrived at the perfection known as me, he gave me one of those toe-curling kisses.

I pulled away, teasingly, and thrust my gift between us. Oh, there'd be time for the other kind of thrusting later, but I couldn't resist. I could not wait to give him his gift. The sexy little I-won-this-round gift.

"Can't it wait?" He bit my earlobe gently and whispered, "I'll open it later."

Lord, it was hard to hang onto any semblance of rational thought with his breath warm in my ear, but somehow I managed.

"Come on, Dylan. Humor me."

"Okay, a newspaper guy walks into a bar and shouts, 'Bartender, I'm looking for your nine-inch pianist.'"

I smacked him. "Stop."

"You heard that one?"

"Heard it? I'm the one who told it to you." I slammed the gift into his chest. "Open it, Foreman."

He unwrapped the package quickly.

"Er, socks? Again with the socks?"

I waggled my eyebrows.

"This makes 36 pairs you've given me since November."

Best girlfriend ever. That's what he had to be thinking.

I'd gotten him some awesome dress socks for Christmas. Imported ones, no less. Because hey, socks are just that sexy. Right up there with nubby rubber thimbles.

Dylan looked bewildered as he gazed down at the gift. He scratched his head.

Ha! I loved it when he pretended like that. Just another little game we play. That he wasn't just as turned on as I was right about then, looking at those six pairs of socks, so neatly folded, so perfectly lined up in the cellophane-wrapped box. Maybe we could take them out of the box and Dylan could try them on for me. One by one by...one.

"Yeah." I gave him my most provocative smile, inadvertently whistling through my teeth (because my provocative smile is a tight one). "Brown ones. Stretchy, ribbed, brown socks."

I wanted to jump his bones—one in particular—right then and there. "Do you like them?"

"I love them." He set them back down on the desk and pulled me in close for a full body hug.

"I win," I murmured against his neck. "Best gift ever."

He nuzzled back, laying a hand on my left breast while pulling my hips closer to his. "Is that right?"

"Why, Mr. Foreman," I whispered into his ear. "Is that a hoagie in your pocket, or are you glad to see me?"

Please say hoagie; please say hoagie. We can pick up where we left off later.

Yes, I'd skipped breakfast again.

He chuckled. "No, it's not a hoagie in my pocket, but I am very glad to see you."

To prove it even more eloquently, he pressed himself against me all the closer. Through the rough material of his jeans, I could feel his growing desire.

Actually, I felt it in a couple places.

What the heck? He'd had only one penis the last time I checked. And I'm a private detective after all; I'm pretty sure I wouldn't have missed a second one!

I backed up and looked down at Dylan's crotch.

He did that little adjusty thing guys do with their jeans when they've got a semi, pulling the material away from the rising action. Then he reached into the right pocket of his jeans.

"Happy three months anniversary, Dix."

And dammit, there was that one-up smile again as I accepted the card. Immediately, he reached for his back pocket and pulled out another envelope. A suspiciously bright red one.

"Happy Valentine's Day too."

Crap! Valentine's Day.

"Surely you didn't forget V-Day?" he said.

"Of course not!" I opened the package of socks, took out three pair. "These three are the Valentine's Day ones. The other three are the anniversary gift. I just...economized on the wrapping. Times are challenging, you know. Everyone's cutting back a little. Consumer confidence is down and all that." I pumped my fist in the air. "Down with overpackaging. Power to the people."

He didn't buy it. I could tell by the look on his face. I lowered my eyes first.

"Dammit!" I thumped the socks down and grabbed the cards from his hands. "Why's it never about me?"

Sulkily, I took the Valentine card and ripped it open. It was cute but not mushy, thank God. Sweet, but nothing that meant we'd have to start calling each other Honey Bunny or anything like that.

Dylan's actual gift to me was even more prettily wrapped than mine had been. And I must admit, I was intrigued by the long, slender tube. Odd packaging, but…

I started unwrapping.

A necklace? A tennis bracelet? Oh, something shiny always rocks! Maybe it was a pen/pencil set, an inscribed one. I'd told Dylan all about those superhero stories I wanted to write. Maybe he'd gotten me a pen set to encourage my literary endeavors. Or maybe—

"It's a dick." I looked up at him. "You gave me a penis for a present? A *plastic*, fake penis?

Yes, in retrospect the emphasis on *plastic* may have been a little odd.

"Well, this is not just your ordinary, everyday plastic penis."

"I can see that. This is nothing like my ordinary, everyday—" Shutting up now.

He reached to take the object out of my hands.

"Oh for God's sake, Dix, let go."

I let go.

"It's a FUD," he explained.

"A what?"

"A female urination device. It lets you pee standing up. I mean, why squat when you can stand?"

I gasped. "Where did you ever buy such a thing?" I was thinking Stoner Stan's. But I'm quite sure Stanley would have mentioned Dylan being in there.

"Where else? The internet."

Okay, I'm pretty open-minded when it comes to all kinds of stuff. Fun. Games. Toys. Socks. And don't get me started on my DVD collection (some people think rent is expensive). But that little item that Dylan just handed me wasn't going into the pleasure drawer of my night stand—like even if there was room in that deep, deep drawer. However, I had been meaning to put in a second night stand…

"Why don't we just share the socks?"

"No, really, this is great. Let me show you how it works."

The shock must have shown on my face.

"I mean, let me take it out of the wrapping." Dylan removed it from its packaging. "See? You place this end with the big opening...there," he gave a guy nod to my nether region, "and then…"

The usually eloquent Mr. Foreman was suddenly lost for

words. The poor guy actually looked flustered.

Yes, I should have rescued him. I should've let him know that I got it. That I understood the mechanics of the thing in my hand. I should have done that.

"Go on," I said.

"Maybe you could read the insert," he suggested.

"The insert?" I held the FUD up to eye level for closer examination.

"The directions." Face flaming now, he handed me the small folded pamphlet. "Read the directions."

"I'll do that."

I wouldn't do that. I crumpled the slip of paper and shoved it in a pocket, to be jettisoned as soon as Dylan was out of sight. I didn't mean to seem unappreciative. Sure, it's the thought that counts and all that. But did I mention I got him *socks*?

"I thought you'd like it," he said. "I've been on enough stake-outs with you to know that you hate having to run behind bushes to pee. Or over to the bus station. Or use one of those blue portable things. Hey, remember that time you climbed onto that warehouse roof and hadn't noticed the security cam—"

"Okay! I get it."

"The point is I *hear* you."

"Serves me right for tinkling so loudly, I guess."

"No, I mean I hear you cursing about it all the time. You've said it more than once: the one and only advantage men have over women is our ability to pee standing up. This device lets you pee standing up."

Why couldn't I have told him the one advantage men have over women is the excess of hundred dollar bills in their lives?

Dylan sighed.

I was starting to feel kind of bad for him. I didn't want to hurt his feelings. And it was a thoughtful—if totally bizarre—gift. I had a boyfriend who actually listened to the things I said, even when they were less than my usual charming words of wisdom. He'd really tried. The least I could do was to really try too.

So I looked the device over. Turned it around in my hand. Held it up, spy glass like, to get a different perspective. Well, it wasn't the most ingenious thing I'd ever seen, but it would work. It really would. No more running around the sides of houses, dropping my drawers just as the blare of yard lights came on to shine off my lily white butt. Really, it was...okay.

Oh, who was I kidding? It was a plastic dick!

"You don't like it," Dylan said.

"No, no, it's great." I shoved it in my oversized purse.

"So?" Dylan said. "I win?"

"Well, I wouldn't go that far." I gestured again to the socks. "Those are warm."

"Perfect, I can wear them this weekend when we go camping with my friends." He marked me with an earnest look. A very starting-up-the-discussion-all-over-again look.

Three of Dylan's law school buddies and two of their spouses (whom he'd never met) were going camping in a few days. Winter camping. Dylan and I had been invited to join them.

No, not deep in the woods with the moose and the bears and all that. But in a nice warm chalet overlooking a small lake. Skating, sledding, bonfire beside the frozen lake, beverages stuck in the snow bank. Heaven, you say? Well, it would be if it were just Dylan and me. But with his friends—his much-younger-than-me friends—I felt strange about it.

It wasn't that we were keeping our romance a secret. But going out with his friends was a bridge we hadn't crossed yet. And I wasn't sure I was ready to.

"I can't go camping," I said. "I have allergies."

"Only to tofu, and actually, Dix, I think it's an aversion more than—"

"What about my REM sleep disorder?"

"We'll have the upper loft all to ourselves. Besides, I've lived through nights of your thrashing around the bed in your sleep before." He waggled his eyebrows suggestively. "And when you were awake too."

So he had.

This was getting desperate. Well, *I* was getting desperate. "Camping's unsafe. Someone might wander into the woods and get attacked by a bobcat, or get impaled by...a loose icicle. Oh, someone might stumble onto an open well and fall in."

He chuckled. "Geez, again with the well. What is it with you and wells lately?" He was trying to keep the discussion serious but light. Yet I could feel the tension in him. The deflation in his eyes. He wanted this.

"Dylan, can we please talk about the camping trip later?"

"I'd like to talk about it now, Dix. Come on, I haven't seen these guys in years, and I've never met Jack's and Chevy's spouses. They're in town for the weekend only, and the cottage is already rented. After the scandal when I got disbarred, most of my law school classmates turned their backs on me. I was suddenly the black sheep of the grad class. Jack, Chevy, and Saffron didn't."

Dylan's disbarment was still a sore spot. A chip on the shoulder he wouldn't—shouldn't—deny. He had turned a child abuser over to the police, before the lowlife could abuse again. Noble? Damned straight it was. But that wasn't the way the client saw it, nor the law society. And it sure as hell wasn't how the high-powered, high-dollar law firm where Dylan had been working saw it. They didn't just fire him—they did one hell of a job spinning his reputation into the gutter. That's when he'd turned to private detective work. That was how we'd met.

"Dix, these people are important to me. I want them to meet you." Those brown eyes darkened. "You're my *girlfriend*."

Damn. I could see how much he wanted this. And yet, I shrugged.

"I want to take this further." He raked a hand through his hair. "I want to take *us* further. And I want—"

There was a pounding on the door. Rapid, frantic. Someone was in a panic. Clearly in dire need.

Oh thank you! A legitimate interruption.

I launched to get the door and get away from the conversation.

"We'll talk more about this later," Dylan said. "I really want this one. I've met your mother. We've gone out with Rochelle and Richard a few times. I really want you to take that leap of faith on us."

"What if that leap lands me in a well?" I said.

He gave me that curious look. "This is getting weird."

I hesitated and nodded. Then I went for the door before the beveled glass hit the floor under those pounding fists. "Let me innnnnnnnnnn!" The doorknob rattled under a very determined grip.

And yet I froze at the sound. Oh damn. Double damn. I knew that voice.

"Aw, hell," Dylan grumbled. Obviously, he recognized the unexpected visitor too. "This can't be good."

I unlocked the door and stepped out of the way in one fluid movement, as Elizabeth Bee swept into the room.

Well, technically it was more of a charge through the doorway than a sweep. And technically, it was Elizabeth Bee-Drammen now, young bride of geriatric hotel mogul Hugh Drammen.

The two of them had kicked that half-your-age-plus-nine rule to the curb. And then beat it with a great big stick. Drammen had at least fifty years on Elizabeth. And yet, from what I'd heard, he was happy, and she was happy. It was a win-win. He had his buxom, beautiful bride, and she had her sugar daddy. So why does the rest of the world get to judge them? People pooh-pooh it when they see it in the tabloids—Anna Nicole and all that. But really, if two people are happy, so what?

Wish my life could be so simple.

But why was Elizabeth there at our office? Perhaps all

wasn't so perfect in Elizabeth's newlywed world. She looked frazzled. Worried. Scared.

I couldn't help but know there was trouble. Big trouble.

How did I know, you ask? How am I just that amazingly brilliant? So very insightful?

Second-to-none investigative skills—I haz them. It's one of the reasons I'm such a kick-ass detective. That combined with my keen intuition, means that little—nay, *nothing*—escapes me. Elizabeth had that flicker of desperation in her eyes. There was a tightness in her demeanor. A hardness in her breath. Oh, and she greeted Dylan and me with, "There's trouble. Big trouble. You've got to help me!"

See? Nothing escapes me.

"What's going on?" I asked.

"It's my husband! Something's happened to Hugh! Something terrible."

Like I said, Hugh Drammen is of an advanced age. So, naturally, the first thing I thought of was a stroke.

Then I shook my head. Knowing Elizabeth, she did a lot more than just stroke him.

Elizabeth sniff-sniff-sniffed back the tears. I handed her an opened box of tissues, one of many we keep around the office.

"I...I think someone's trying to kill Hugh!" she sobbed. "I'm worried over my sweet...my sweet..." She couldn't finish. Those sniff, sniffs turned into tears, tears.

Dylan was moved by the waterworks. He's always the softie.

Okay, maybe I was a little moved too. Elizabeth really looked shaken up. People change; people have the right to change. Maybe Elizabeth had done so. Maybe what she felt for Hugh wasn't exclusively a sugar-daddy sort of love.

"You're worried over your sweet husband?" Dylan said. "Is that what you were going to say, Elizabeth? The only man you've ever really loved?"

"Yes, right." She nodded in a good-idea way and blew her nose. "Sweet husband. The only man I've ever loved and all that. But I'm also worried about my sweet two million dollars!" She tossed her head back and wailed.

Dylan and I looked at each other.

Oh boy. This case would be a doozie.

I didn't have the details yet. Didn't have a bead on all the particulars. But just that finger-snapping quickly, I had a name for the case. I knew Elizabeth. I knew the stakes. And I knew—oh, how I knew!—we'd be covering her assets.

CHAPTER 2

I POURED THREE COFFEES, one for each of us.

By this point, you've probably ascertained that Elizabeth Bee-Drammen and I have a history. And you would have ascertained correctly. We'd met months before, when I'd been working on another case, The Case of the Flashing Fashion Queen. She'd proven to be a valuable resource, full of information. For a price, of course.

Our association had continued when Dylan and I infiltrated a local cuddle club and—surprise, surprise—found her there with her then-future, now-current husband, Hugh Drammen.

Were Elizabeth and I close? Heck no. But I had to wonder who really was close to Elizabeth. Who really knew her?

I had gone to Elizabeth's and Hugh's wedding, but I'd kept a low profile. Good decision, as it turned out. I spotted two former 'marks'—wealthy, cheating wives I'd nabbed not too long before. I thought they might not greet me with open arms. Which is okay by me, considering I'm the anti-touchy-feely person. But I'd sat at the back, skipped the receiving line, and gave the guest book a pass.

The wedding was lavish for a justice of the peace affair, especially considering how quickly it was put together. But

Hugh Drammen was a man used to getting what he wanted, when he wanted it.

I knew the history: Hugh and his late-brother, Prosser, had started with a couple of motels in the early sixties. They had expanded to twenty by the time the seventies rolled around. All of them prosperous. With Prosser's untimely passing—a plane crash—Hugh had inherited full control of the company in 1979. And things had skyrocketed. The Drammen Hotels were not world-famous, but were certainly well known throughout the US and Canada. As was the Drammen name. It was one of those money names. Just like everywhere else on the planet, money gets things done in Marport City.

So regarding the quickie wedding, let me give you a little backdrop. The invitations were printed overnight and hand delivered to those lucky guests via white-gloved courier the very next day. The city's best caterer—Kenny Kent, another acquaintance of mine—doubled his staff for two days to accommodate the Bee-Drammen six-course menu on such short notice. The salmon was flown in from British Columbia. The fresh beef steaks from Alberta. They served up Hall's Harbour lobster. Even the wine was perfect, flown in from a private vineyard in California. Marport City's finest seamstress worked around the clock to get Elizabeth's dream dress ready. And friends and family started arriving within three days of getting that golden ticket invite.

That is, Hugh's friends and family started arriving. Despite a couple of cousins crashing Elizabeth's bridal shower (such as it was), no Bees descended on the wedding.

By all appearances, most were thrilled to be there. Some people just like weddings. Others go for the desserts—guilty as charged—and some are just that curious. And who wouldn't want to get a gander at the new Mrs. Drammen in her lavish wedding dress?

Still, it was obvious to me that at least a few attendees did not want to be there. There were polite-but-tight grins galore. And you know how I like to eavesdrop—

"My land, he's an old fool." I heard that sentiment a few times. Almost as many times as the words "gold digger" whispered through the gathering.

Hugh flew Prosser's only offspring, Morris, in all the way from Cold Bay, Alaska. He came alone, looking older than the forty-some years Hugh's only nephew had to be. There was an unease to Morris. He looked uncomfortable in his very skin, not to mention the clothes he'd donned for the wedding. Morris kept pulling at the cuffs of his ill-fitting suit, sticking a finger in the collar of his pressed white shirt, and turning his head as if it were choking him.

Hugh's daughter Tammy Drammen, her too-tanned husband, Allen Boyden, and their bubbly, early-twenties daughter, Roma Drammen, were in the wedding party. I saw their names on the program. And I learned more as I listened to the chit-chat around me.

Tammy and Allen lived with Hugh. No, not in a guest house on the premises or even in their own wing within the monster-sized mansion. Their bedrooms—yep, separate—were just down the hall from Hugh and Elizabeth's. Apparently Hugh wanted everyone close and cozy.

Roma was in her second year of university, studying bio-chem. On the fast-track to becoming a doctor. An anesthesiologist like her mother, no less. She lived in Toronto, where she studied, but naturally came home for her grandfather's wedding. Her parents were dressed conservatively—tuxedo for Allen, Tammy in a subtle grey-blue gown. Roma, on the other hand, was dressed in a very form-fitting animal print sheath that revealed long legs and peep-toed platform shoes. The dress also dipped in the back to show a tasteful but fairly large tattoo. Not exactly wedding attire.

Roma's last name was Drammen, which, naturally, made me wonder if Allen was Roma's dad. I didn't wonder long. They looked too much alike to be anything other than father and daughter.

But where were Elizabeth's family and friends? No mother or doting grandmother? No hot younger sisters, hunky brothers, pull-my-finger uncles, half-cut cousins, close-to-perfect aunts who never forgot a birthday? None of the above. There wasn't even a best friend from way back. I found it more curious than sad. But then of course, I remembered what Elizabeth had told the gang at the Cuddle Club. She was practically all alone in the world: fatherless, with a mother who was a full-fledged cougar, and a little old grandmother who'd practically raised her.

How much of that was crap?

Only Elizabeth knew.

Yes, Dylan had been invited too, but because of a case we were working, we couldn't both go. So while he got to stake out the local drug dealer's house to see if our client's fifteen-year-old son dropped by that fine Saturday afternoon, I got to go to the wedding. Elizabeth looked gorgeous. Happy. The entire family did.

I watched the ceremony and got out of there before the reception. But not before sneaking into the kitchen for a slice of Kenny's chocolate cheesecake.

Elizabeth hadn't spoken two words to me at the wedding, but I knew she'd seen me there.

And as she stood there in our offices, I wondered all over again why she had bothered to invite me at all. Was it a friendly thing? Or did she know even then that she'd be needing our help? That our services might come in handy someday?

"That second thing, Dix," Elizabeth said through her drying tears and all-done snuffles. "That your services might come in handy someday. Yes, that's mostly why I invited you."

Whoops. Guess I'd wondered that aloud.

"No offence," she said.

"None taken." And that was the truth.

Despite the crying, Elizabeth looked like a million bucks. Wonderful French manicure, professionally coifed hair and tailored dress revealing her stunning décolletage. That Prada tote and matching pumps were definitely not of the Wal-Mart variety. Apparently, she was wasting no time adjusting to a lifestyle she could now afford.

Good for her.

"Have a seat," I said.

Dylan handed the distressed damsel another tissue as we settled into his office. Okay, technically it was the reception area.

Dylan had graduated to full-fledged PI, but he still occupied the outer office he'd used when he was my assistant. Space—or more accurately, the extra rent said space would command—had always been an issue. I'd started this practice on a shoestring with a conservative fiscal plan to build the business. Then Dylan had showed up, and I'd hired him on the spot, throwing my business plan into a spin. Thankfully, he didn't seem to mind the lack of a private office. And it wasn't like we could afford a receptionist. That said, we often talked about moving the office again someday, putting out the Dodd-Foreman Private Investigators shingle in a different locale.

Blow-Up Betty vacated her hold on the old couch as I sat down. And by vacated, I mean I picked her up and tossed her behind the couch—and not without some satisfaction. Maybe it was just me, but Betty seemed to be assuming more presence around our office. A pale plastic foot stuck up in the air as she fell face first. Ha! I could just picture that look of surprise on her perpetually open mouth. With a backhanded bat, I knocked the foot away. It came back up and smacked me in the eye.

See what I mean? Attitude!

"Do you need a little help with that?" Elizabeth asked.

Reluctantly, I nodded. And winked. Man, that foot smack had hurt!

Elizabeth jumped up on her knees on the cushion, shoved Betty safely and securely down against the wall, and turned back around. She flopped into sitting position again.

Dylan sat down behind his desk. He pulled a yellow legal pad from the top drawer. "Last time I saw you, Elizabeth," he said, "you were celebrating your engagement to Hugh at the Cuddle Club."

She nodded thoughtfully. "Happier times, Dylan. Happier times."

"So what's up?" I asked.

She drew a deep breath. With a hand on her chest, she landed a perfect count-to-three dramatic pause and then rushed right ahead with: "Someone's trying to kill Hugh."

"Did you call the police?" That seemed to me like the reasonable first question to ask.

"No, Hugh-Bear doesn't want me to. He...he's not taking this seriously at all."

Ugh. Still with the Hugh-Bear.

"Tell us about it," Dylan said. He grabbed a pen, clicking it ready.

Me? I didn't get ready to take any notes. Purposefully. Dylan would get the details down. I'd do my own doodling later, if it was indeed a doodle-worthy situation. But I wanted him to know I trusted him. Compensation for my reluctance in other areas of our relationship? The camping trip, for instance.

Maybe.

Elizabeth began, "Last night there was a fire at the house, in my husband's study. Nothing that we needed to call the fire department about, but it could have been serious. Thankfully, Morris was there. He smelled the smoke and managed to put out the fire."

"Morris?" I interrupted, "He's still around? I would have thought he'd be back up in Alaska by now."

Elizabeth shrugged, lightly. "He decided to stay in Marport City a while longer. He's all alone, no family or close friends. We—Hugh and I—need some things fixed up around the house. Morris knows all about antique repair and restoration, so we asked him to stay on for a bit."

Yep, I caught it. *We* asked him to stay for a bit. I've never known Elizabeth to do much of anything unless it was to her advantage. Why did it suit her to have Morris around?

Dylan said, "Good thing he was there, huh?"

"You've got that right." There was that smile again.

"So you don't think this fire was an accident?" I said.

"No," Elizabeth said. "I'm sure it wasn't."

"How so?"

"Like I said, it was in Hugh's study. He was the only one there, and Hugh hasn't smoked in years. Actually, no one smokes in the house. Hugh hates it. Tracy, that was Hugh's first wife, died from lung cancer. He's not a very strict man, but he absolutely won't allow smoking. That's a big house rule."

"Could a candle have started the fire?" I asked.

She shook her head. "No."

"Electrical?"

"No, Dix. Wiring was checked just two weeks ago."

Dylan's eyes sharpened. "Any particular reason to be checking out the electrical wiring?"

"It was just part of the appraisal I ordered on the house. Can you believe it hasn't been appraised in years?"

Ah, classic Elizabeth. She'd probably had every object in the house valued as well, including the antique furniture Morris was apparently restoring.

"What about a spark from the fireplace?" Dylan asked.

"There is a fireplace in Hugh's study, but it's never lit. Humphrey—that's Hugh's dog—is terrified of fire. He's a rescue dog. Hugh got him from the local SPCA. The ugliest mutt you've ever seen and scared of his own shadow. He was already old when Hugh got him, and he's getting blinder and deafer by the day. But Hugh absolutely loves him. Anyway, fire really sends Humphrey through the roof. Hugh thinks the poor dog must have been abused when he was a pup to be so terrified of it now."

"People can be jerks," Dylan said.

Silently, I agreed. Cruel and stupid jerks.

"So how do you think the fire in the study started?" I asked.

"Someone set it," Elizabeth said, her voice ringing with conviction. "I just don't know who."

That was the bullet question. Some like to call it the "million dollar question," but until I actually have that million dollar case, bullet it is. It wasn't just the verbal answer I was watching for. I was looking for clues. Would Elizabeth hesitate? Would she hedge? Did she know more than she was telling Dylan and me? Would she tell us everything upfront and willingly, or would I have to drag it out of her?

"Do you know who *didn't* set it?" I asked.

"Morris was with me in my study," she said. "Thankfully, too, because he's the one who smelled the smoke. We can vouch for each other."

My turn to smile.

So there it was: our Miss Elizabeth had been a busy little bee.

She rolled her eyes at me. "It's not what you're thinking, Dix."

She must have seen the doubt on my face.

"And remember," Elizabeth said, "If you take this case, you'll be working for me, Dix Dodd. Not the other way around."

"Fair enough."

Elizabeth had a good point. But I wasn't just being cynical. I'd been in this business too long not to think "not what you're thinking" was often exactly what I should be thinking. However, there was no reason to argue the point now. Another thing I'd learned from years in the business: get paid first, argue those points later.

"And while you and Morris were vouching for each other," I said, "what was your new hubby doing? Where was

Hugh-Bear during this time?"

"Every evening, at exactly seven o'clock, Hugh retires to his study. I pour him a beer, and the housekeeper, Caryn, fixes him up a snack plate. He takes both to his sofa and settles in to read."

"Beer?" Hugh didn't strike me as a beer man, though, admittedly, my opinion of him just went up a notch.

"Yes. I pour him one cold Guinness Original. He has a small bar in his study, and the cooler is set to seven degrees Celsius. And the beer has to be poured slowly into the Oktoberfest mug he got in Germany in 1977. He'll read ten pages of whatever book he's into and then sleep for an hour or so."

"The snack tray?" Dylan asked.

"Seven saltines topped with Edam cheese. Seven gherkin pickles. It's all for Humphrey actually. Well, the cheese and crackers. Hugh eats the pickles. Anyway, that's it till the grandfather clock in the hallway strikes nine o'clock, and Hugh re-emerges from the study. My husband is very, very set in his ways."

Set in his ways? Her husband was very, very OCD!

No, I don't have a degree in psychology or any such thing. I'm not a doctor nor do I play one on TV. Off TV? Well, there was that one time Dylan and I... Never mind.

But believe it or not, I could kind of understand Hugh's OCD. For some people, there is a genuine comfort to order, to routine. And a genuine discomfort with the unpredictable. There's a sense of security in the same time, same place, same people sort of thing. Yes, honestly, I got it that Hugh wanted his Guinness served at seven degrees Celsius every night at seven o'clock, but then something struck me as odd.

"Every night?" I asked, arching an eyebrow at the loaded suggestion.

"You're wondering about the evenings Hugh and I spent at the Cuddle Club."

"Right."

"Hugh made an exception. And he made it for me. We met at the Bombay Spa. Last summer he pulled a muscle and needed some gentle massage therapy for his back. I assisted with his massages."

"I bet you made sure of it," I said.

"Absolutely. Every time." Elizabeth smiled with satisfaction.

I smiled with admiration. Gotta love it when a woman unapologetically goes after what she wants.

"But after that first time we met, Hugh started booking his massages around the times I was working. That's how well we hit it off. And then I convinced him to meet me for Cuddle Club. I wanted to get closer. To get to know him better. Hugh wanted the same. Caryn told me that first night we went to Cuddle Club was the first time in ten years—since his first wife died—that he skipped his seven o'clock Guinness routine."

Elizabeth was pleased with herself—with her powers of feminine persuasion. Or just...dare I say it?...happy that her husband really had been that smitten with her.

"So while Hugh has his nightly beer, what do you do?" Dylan asked.

She shrugged. "I usually go into my own study. It's just across the hall from his. It belonged to Tracy, and now it belongs to me." She turned to me. "You should see it, Dix. The high oak walls, the paneled ceilings, the Persian rug that covers half the floor. Hugh said I could fix it up any way I wanted. That it and everything in it was mine now. A wedding gift."

"What do you study?"

She looked at me as if I'd just asked the stupidest question possible.

"Online shopping."

Turns out I *had* just asked the stupidest question possible. Then I asked the second stupidest question possible. "Did you ever shop for a FUD? You know a female urination—"

Dylan interrupted with a cough and a legitimate question. Well, at least a slightly more legitimate question. "And you were there the night of the fire, right?"

"Right."

"But not shopping?" I put in. "I mean, with Morris there—"

"No, I wasn't shopping, but we're getting off topic. This is about the fire that could have killed my husband, not what I do with my private time when my husband is enjoying his. Like I said, *I* am paying *you guys*."

"Where was everyone else?" I asked.

"Tammy and Allen had gotten into one of their stupid arguments a couple hours before. Who knows what it was about this time? But I think they were upstairs in their bedrooms—their separate bedrooms. I heard two doors slamming. Roma's away at university. It was in the evening, so the day staff—Lois and Glori—were gone. Caryn, the live-in housekeeper, was there, but she was outside when the fire started."

"Where outside?" Dylan asked.

"Oh, wandering the yard—taking her evening stroll along the trails. She came charging in through the patio door of Hugh's study when the fire alarm finally sounded. She tripped over poor old Humphrey and nearly fell flat on her face. But thankfully, Morris already had the fire out, and it was just smoldering." Elizabeth tossed a dismissive hand. "Caryn's an odd one too. Hugh collects them, you know."

"What? Housekeepers? Like, in a binder or something?"

"No, odd ones, Dix. Charity cases. Though don't ever use that term around him. My husband has a heart of gold. Oh, and don't look at me like I've got a gold-digging shovel to go along with it. You know what I mean."

I had something else to chew on just then. "Could Hugh have started that fire himself?"

From across the room, I caught it: Dylan's little nod.

"No way." Elizabeth was adamant. "He wouldn't. Not by

accident or design. Hugh is far from senile. And he's not depressed—nothing like that. And even if he were inclined to set something on fire, he'd never, ever traumatize Humphrey like that, let alone put the old mutt in any kind of danger."

Hmm, whoever *did* set the fire apparently didn't much care what happened to the poor old dog.

"So you want me to find out how that fire got started?"

"Yes, I want you to figure out who started it," Elizabeth said. "And I want something else."

Ah, there it was. Of course there was more to it. Hadn't I had that niggle and nudge of intuition?

"What would that be?" Dylan asked.

"I want you to cover my ass." Elizabeth's gaze shifted from me to Dylan and back again. "There's a pre-nup. If Hugh lives ten years after we're married, I get fifty percent of his fortune. The rest gets divided up within the family."

Dylan whistled. "A good-sized chunk of change, I imagine."

"Definitely," Elizabeth said. "But if he dies before our ten-year anniversary, it gets a little wonky."

Ah, wonky. One of my favorite technical terms. Covers so much, yet so little. "Meaning?"

"Every six months off that magical clock, I lose a significant percentage. Significant."

"And if your Hugh-Bear died too soon..."

"Nothing before a year. Just the clothes on my back and any gifts he gives me during our marriage."

So another reason for the love of online shopping. If Elizabeth were to leave with just the clothes on her back, she'd be wearing layers of Versace and a mother lode of jewels.

My gaze went to her left hand where the giant four-and-a-half carat emerald-cut diamond in question glittered in its platinum setting. I remembered it well. It had temporarily disappeared at Elizabeth's bachelorette party when she'd taken it off for the festivities in the Bee family tradition. Poor

Elizabeth's consternation had been complete when she discovered it had gone missing. Fortunately, I was in attendance at that bachelorette party—hey, who do you think organized the stripper?—and was able to solve it. I called that case Gone in a Flash.

"Well," I said, "I can't really see anyone trying to take your engagement ring from you."

She huffed. "Are you kidding? It's worth well over a hundred thousand dollars, Dix. But, even if it were worth a buck twenty five, my dear step daughter would chop it off my hand rather than see me keep it."

I blinked. "Wait a minute, are you talking about Tammy? She looked so happy for you and her dad at the wedding."

"That was then. She changed right after the wedding." Elizabeth sighed. "I've got nine months to go before any real money kicks in. Nine long months. So if anything happens to Hugh before that, I don't get a dime."

Just that quickly, just that genuinely, the tears were falling again.

Dylan couldn't help himself. He was across the room in an instant, placing a comforting hand on her shoulder.

"And besides, you love your husband, right, Elizabeth?" he asked.

"Sure, sure. That too."

After a few sniff-sniffs back, Elizabeth said, "So you see why I need your help."

"Yes," I answered.

"Will you take the case, Dix? Dylan?" She looked at each of us in turn.

"You want us to find out who started that fire?" Dylan said.

"Yes, and make sure nothing bad happens to my husband until we do get to the bottom of this."

Oh boy. Elizabeth Bee-Drammen wanted not only a couple of top-of-the-line PIs, but bodyguards for the old guy too.

Every fiber of my body told me it wasn't a great idea. It screamed that this was a case to be passed up. Even as I watched her wiping away the tears, I reminded myself that Elizabeth was trouble. Trouble with a capital T.

Then she opened that Prada purse and handed over a big roll of cash.

Not a promise of payment. Not a post-dated check written on someone else's account. No expired or forged gift-cards. Elizabeth handed over a nice, tight roll of good old-fashioned hundred dollar bills.

"Fifteen of them," she said.

"Need a receipt?" I asked.

She shook her head. "Of course not."

That told me bucket-loads too. "So Hugh and the rest of the family—?"

"Do not know I'm hiring you. Right," Elizabeth confirmed. "Tammy doesn't like outsiders in the house. And besides, it'll be easier for you to investigate if no one knows you're a private eye."

Ah, crap.

"Well, Hugh's met me, Elizabeth," I said.

"You can stuff your bra."

"Yeah, well you can just shove a pineapple—"

"No. Seriously. You're pretty flat-chested, and then there is this whole gravity-over-forty thing. But you know all about that!"

Dylan snorted a laugh and then hid it—poorly—behind another coughing fit.

"Catching a cold, Dylan?" I grated.

"Seem to be."

If Elizabeth felt the effects of my death-gaze boring into her, she didn't show it. If there were any justice in the world, her head would have started smoking any minute. But said head stayed smoke-free, a fact that would no doubt please Humphrey.

Unscathed, Elizabeth continued. "Hugh isn't senile, like I said, but he really isn't that...people observant."

"Face blindness?"

"Not quite, but close. And he's a boob man." As if we needed a demonstration on just what a boob man would be interested in, Elizabeth straightened her back and shoved out her chest.

"And the rest of the family? I was at the wedding, Elizabeth," I said.

"Right." She smiled. "No one saw you. I knew you'd arrive late, sit at the back, and sneak away as soon as you got an eyeful and some cheesecake. But at least you would know the lay of the land. Get a feel for things."

I was getting the picture.

So was Dylan.

"And Tammy doesn't like outsiders in the house." I repeated. "But since we've never met, you can pass me off as a family friend. A relative."

"Actually," she said. "I was thinking I could pass you off as my mother. You had me young."

Mother? Elizabeth wanted me to pose as her frickin' *mother?*

Dylan laughed. "Congratulations, Dix. It's a girl!"

I gave him the death-ray glare.

Damn, still no smoldering.

"Oh, and because I told everyone you like your young stuff," Elizabeth continued, "that'll get Dylan in too. You can bring him along as your flavor of the month."

Mmm, Dylan-flavored. Right up there with chocolate.

"No way!" Dylan said.

My turn to snort a laugh. "Congratulations, Dylan. It's a boy! Boy toy, that is. And it's *you*."

Whoops. I'd spoken too soon. Considering the age gap between us, I should have thought that one out before opening my mouth.

"Hugh will recognize me," Dylan pointed out. "I'm guessing this boob man of yours wasn't looking at *my* cleavage."

She sighed. "Honestly, I wasn't kidding about that near

face blindness thing. Give him a financial spread sheet, cost analysis, business prospectus, and he'll remember ever figure and word. Pore over it for hours. But with people, not so much. He went to the Cuddle Club because I wanted him to go with me, and"—she indicated her boobs with an aren't–these-amazing gesture—"he only had eyes for me."

"We got it," I said. "Boob man."

"Yes." Elizabeth smiled. "Aren't you glad your cleavage is so unremarkable, Dix? That must be a bonus in your line of work."

"Whoa, there," Dylan said, jumping to my defense. "Everyone's cleavage is unremarkable compared to yours, Elizabeth."

"Dylan!"

"What?" He glanced at me. "Oh, shit. I didn't mean it like that. All I meant to say was Elizabeth has great breasts and you shouldn't feel bad because—"

I glared at him, and he wisely shut up.

Okay, back to Hugh Drammen. So we had beer, financial figures, charity cases, and big breasts. The guy had his obsessions. I was starting to get a very clear picture of the man.

"He's the kindest soul I've ever met, Dix," Elizabeth said. "But definitely a little on the strange side."

Dylan frowned. "Still, Elizabeth, I don't know that I can pull it off."

"Wear a fake moustache, if you're worried about it," she said. "What do they call those big, bushy ones?"

"Porn staches! Dylan, you get to wear a porn stache!" I said, a little too excitedly. Or maybe it was the squeal and hand clapping after I said it that betrayed my exuberance. Or the jumping up and down on the couch.

What the hell? Who put a squeaker box in Betty?

Dylan shook his head. "You may as well sit down, Dix. I'm not in."

I sat down.

I mouthed the words, “Fifteen hundred dollars.” Then, because I knew Elizabeth was watching my moving lips, I added, “As a down payment." And then, as further insurance, I added, “Partner.”

What could Dylan say to that? I had him by the short and curlies.

He agreed to go along with it.

“One more thing,” Elizabeth said. “We’ll need a loving grandma. Any sweet little old lady should do. Do you know one?”

Dylan and I exchanged a glance. Did we ever.

We both knew who we’d recruit, and she was far from sweet.

“Don’t worry, Elizabeth,” I said. “The four of us will take care of everything.”

Elizabeth cocked her head. “*Four* of you?”

“Yeah. Dylan, me...and my substandard breasts.”

Dylan dropped his head.

Oh, yeah, he’d be paying for this.

CHAPTER 3

THERE WERE A few details to be worked out before Elizabeth Bee-Drammen—why do I always think *we-be-jammin'* when I say that?—left the office.

And work them out, we did.

We would arrive at the Drammen estate that very evening. It was a honking big house on the western outskirts of Marport City. Elizabeth, Dylan, and I agreed on D—just D—for my undercover name. I like to keep it simple and close to my real name. For Dylan, we decided on Magnus because, well, Dylan liked it. I wanted him to go with Rod, or Lance, or Buck, but I was overruled.

And the granddaddy of all details to be worked out...payment!

Not even haggled over, Elizabeth had agreed right away to the terms Dylan and I put forth. That is, if something happened to Hugh while we were on the clock, we wouldn't receive another dime, and that wad of bills already deposited in my hand—and spent in my mind—would be returned, less our expenses. And once we found out who'd set the fire, keeping Hugh safe in the meantime, we'd get another wad of cash. Twice as big. There were nips and tucks to the agreement to be made if things went over three days.

"Surely it won't go over three days, Dix," Dylan said. "We have plans for the weekend, remember? With Chevy, Jack, and Saffron."

Yeah, right. The camping trip with the law school buddies...how could I forget? Bring on the smores. And vodka. Lots of vodka.

After Elizabeth left, Dylan and I unrolled that wad of under-the-table cash and counted those bills out one more time. Yes, I held every other one up to the light. Dylan scraped a fingernail along a few of those older notes too, but they were definitely legit.

The cash advance was timely. My little Hyundai needed new winter tires. That bundle from Elizabeth was getting them for me. And I owed Dylan six hundred bucks. He wasn't on salary anymore, now that we were partners. My lean times were his lean times and vice versa. But other car repairs had set me back a bit last month, plus I had condo payments since Mom had actually sold the place to me. Dylan had helped me out a bit when I was low on cash.

Partner help? Or boyfriend help?

I wish I knew.

Like I said: weird life.

We were heading west, on our way to the Drammen house. Crunched up in the passenger seat of my little car, Dylan flipped the visor mirror down to get another look at himself as Magnus. He started griping all over again.

"God, this looks stupid. It really is a porn stache, isn't it?" He pulled at the crotch of his too-tight, black jeans. Those were part of the get up too. Yes, my idea.

Hee hee hee.

"It's a fake mustache," I said. "That's all. Don't be such a baby. Just part of the role you're playing. Nothing wrong with some good old-fashioned role-playing"

Role-playing...I could so get into that. Especially if Dylan wore that stache again.

Maybe if I said it often enough, he'd get the hint.

His upper lip twitched into a smile. And as the lip twitched, so did the thick mustache. So did parts of me. Ah, the old twitch and squeeze.

Visions of that mustache tickling up my thighs filled my head. Well, our next "anniversary" was just a month away. He may have gotten me a stand-up-and-pee dick for our happy three months together, but all I wanted now was to feel a mustachioed kiss, skimming up my legs, and—

"Whoa, watch the road!" His hands gripped the dash as my passenger-side tire threatened to hit the roadside gravel.

I swerved back into the centre of the lane. Okay, hands on the wheel; mind on the driving. But since my mouth was currently free…

"I think that stache looks very handsome on you. Very masculine. Very sophisticated. Soooo sexy. You know...with our four-month anniversary coming up, maybe you could grow a real one."

"It makes him look more macho, don't you think?" That was the vote from the backseat.

I'd thought Mrs. Presley was still sleeping. She had been last time I'd checked the fuzzy-dice adorned mirror. Well, she *might* have been sleeping. You just never knew with Mrs. P. She could have been faking it back there, eyes closed, mouth hanging open, head leaning on the hot pink neck pillow, just listening to me and Dylan talking. Gathering intelligence to use against me.

What? Me, paranoid? Not a chance. The lady loves to razz me. It's her passion. I swear it's one of her greatest pleasures in life. And she's damned good at it.

But if she was really in my corner on the whole Dylan growing a for-real mustache…

"I agree one hundred percent. The mustache does lend him

some extra macho, doesn't it?" I said. "Good observation, Mrs. Presley, er, I mean Nanny Jane.

"That's Mother to you, D," she said.

Indeed.

I didn't know how happy Elizabeth would be to see Mrs. Jane Presley in the role of my mother/her grandmother, aka Nanny Jane. After all, Elizabeth had broken the hearts of both of Mrs. P's boys, Cal and Craig. Okay, so they weren't boys, per se. They were full-grown men. Full grown men who still had their mother kiss them goodnight.

Neither son had been pleased when I'd asked for their mother's assistance. But when I told Mrs. P that I needed her help, she hadn't hesitated. Well, more specifically, when I told her I needed help on a case that involved a day or two spent at Hugh Drammen's mansion, where Elizabeth now resided, she'd gone to pack a bag. All of five minutes later—either she's ultra-organized or she keeps one on the ready—she'd started dishing out instructions for the boys about taking care of the place while she was gone.

While Hugh Drammen had invested in a chain of hotels, Mrs. Presley had invested in a single motel when she'd arrived in Marport City years ago, a grieving widow with two small sons in tow. With the insurance money she'd gotten from her husband's death, she'd been quite content with her little place. Still was. The Underwood was a shady spot on the rougher edge of the city than we were heading to now, catering to hookers and johns and those looking for an hour or two in a private room with clean sheets on the bed, an unringing phone, and no questions asked.

Well, most of the time there were no questions asked. As long as everything was on the up and up, that is. If it wasn't, Mrs. P asked a hell of a lot of questions.

If an underage girl walked into the place, she called Social Services. If a john looked dangerous, one hard glare from Mrs. P—backed up by the ever-present Cal or Craig or both—and there wasn't a problem. More than a few women had taken refuge from abusive spouses under her roof. She'd helped them turn their lives around, more than anyone knew. She even dried tears and poured shots of Baileys a time or two.

And I adored her for it.

Dylan thought the world of Mrs. P too, so I pressed for more on the mustache front.

"A nice bushy mustache can make a man look more dignified too," I said. "Don't you find?" I met her gaze in the mirror.

"It kind of does," she agreed. "And you know, it makes him look older. Like, not your-age older but closer to that bar. You must find that appealing. A relief almost."

Dylan snorted a laugh, as I cursed myself under my breath. I'd set myself up for that slam. Mrs. P was practically honor-bound to deliver it.

Chuckling, she said, "Relax, Dix. I'm just getting into character. You know, mother of a floozy."

Floozy – I snorted in the most unladylike way at that word.

"Yes," she went on, "I figure Old Nanny Jane wouldn't be too thrilled with her daughter's transgressions."

Personally, I think transgressions are underrated.

Mrs. P/Nanny Jane sat back in the seat with a smile on her face. I knew the look—the wheels were turning in that little old lady's mind.

"We're going to have so much fun," she said. "I love when I get to come along on cases. Remember that Florida trip we took, the one with the bingo? Wasn't I darned helpful there?"

Darned helpful indeed.

Dylan pointed to a gated driveway on the left. "Is that the place?"

"Yes, that's it." I signaled the left turn and pulled in. I stopped the car at the gate and glanced first to Mrs. P and then Dylan. "Okay, folks," I said. "We're on."

Mrs. P clapped her hands. Dylan twitched his mustache and waggled his eyebrows. He raised his butt off the seat as he pulled at the knees of those too-tight jeans. And not to give his knees the breathing space. The hem of his jeans lifted ever so slightly.

He was wearing them—the brown socks. That's right, brown socks with black jeans, just like in those old black and white movies.

Dylan saw my interest, caught the look in my eyes. He smiled. Yum, that sexy mustache smile…

"The three of us are going to have so much fun!" Mrs. P said.

Like a bucket of cold water thrown from the back seat of the car, that doused any flame stirring up front.

"Drammen Residence." The male voice—presumably the security guard Elizabeth had told us about—came through a box mounted on a pole on my side of the car.

I rolled my window down and identified myself to the disembodied voice as D Bee, Elizabeth's mother. The gates opened slowly but smoothly, and we drove through. A second later, we were passing a small building. That had to be the gatehouse/security guard station.

I glanced at the clock on my dashboard. It was just after seven. Hmm, chances were pretty good that I'd have the case wrapped up in a couple hours. We could be back to Marport City by midnight. Yes, I am that brilliant. But I knew I really should give Mrs. P at least one night in lap of luxury. Right? Or two? No, I wouldn't pad the bill. But if I could stretch it out to the weekend, that would be just long enough so we'd miss the camping trip…

I looked at Dylan inquiringly. "All set?"

"You know it."

"Great," I said. "It's showtime."

Little did I know, it would be one hell of a show.

"This is creepy," Mrs. P undid her seatbelt and leaned forward between Dylan and me, as I cruised up the driveway.

"It looks like something out of a Stephen King novel."

"How do you figure that, Mrs. P?" Dylan asked. He leaned forward to peer through the windshield into the dim depths himself.

"Come on, look around," she said. "Don't you almost expect it? People with pyrokinetic powers locked up inside that huge house, waiting to incinerate us the moment we enter their lair. An evil clown crouched down behind every tree. Demented dogs ready to sink their teeth into you—stuff like that."

"There's a tension, actually." I said. "Yes. That's it. This place strikes me as just...tense."

I'd answered automatically. Instinctively. Intuitively.

I stopped the car. The tick-tick of the engine was the only sound in the complete stillness.

"Maybe they've all left," Mrs. P supplied, obviously referring to the lack of lights on inside the house. "Or maybe they've been killed by a big hulking axe murderer, and he's waiting in there right now for us. Smiling weirdly, his eyes sliding from side to side, as he thinks about adding us to that pile of dead bodies." She nudged me on the shoulder. "Go see, D."

"Too late to back out now, Mother," I said to Mrs. P.

"Back out? I wouldn't dream of it."

Dylan and I got out of the car, and he pulled the seat forward so Mrs. P could climb out of the back. Whereas I had to perform major grunting contortions to crawl out of my little two-door, petite Mrs. Presley slipped out with ease.

"Careful with my bags there, D," she called over her shoulder as she walked toward the door.

"Yes, Mother."

I stood at the back of the car.

"Better do your jeans up, D," Dylan said.

"Right."

Driving in those jeans would have been murder if I hadn't unbuttoned them when we'd left the Underwood motel.

Thankfully, all that sitting had stretched them out momentarily, so I was able to suck my stomach in and pull them closed without employing more drastic measures.

I opened the trunk and picked up the Samsonite Mrs. P had packed. Dylan grabbed our two much smaller bags.

"They've probably got an indoor pool, wouldn't you think?" Mrs. Presley walked toward the door, not waiting for my answer. "I brought my swimsuit just in case. And I hope my room has a balcony like that one." She pointed to a lovely little balcony off a second floor patio door. "Nothing like breakfast on the balcony."

"It's winter, Nanny Jane," I said.

"Oh, I've never minded the cold."

Yeah right! So sayeth the Sweater Queen.

"And you can shovel the snow off in no time, D, as long as you don't take those long breaks you're so fond of. It's getting dark out. But I can hold the flashlight through the window if you want to get started tonight. Well, as long as you push a chair over for me to sit by the door. And get me a blanket. And a tea."

The woman thinks of everything.

Dylan laughed beside me.

And then there was me—bag-lugging me. I smiled. But for a different reason than Mrs. P's proposed foray into luxury at my expense.

I was on a high.

Nowhere near drug or chocolate induced. It was always a thrill beginning a case. Every freakin' time. No matter the circumstance, the adrenaline rushed. The blood pumped. Because the stage was set for me to shine.

And shine I would! I was Dix Dodd, private investigator, about to embark on another case. Living the dream, baby. The sexy partner, the money in my pocket, the payday to come. The adventure. The danger. The Hyundai…

Okay, in my dreams it was an awesome red '67 Mustang, but you get the picture.

Though it had been a long haul getting to this point in my life, I'd made it. Back in the day, I'd hit a few glass ceilings. Yes, I'd tumbled back a step or two along the way. And yes, I had the scars and bumps and bruises to prove that it wasn't always easy. But there I was, nonetheless.

I was there because I deserved to be there.

Dylan, Mrs. P, and I approached the house. And as light spilled through the opening door, I knew that nothing would stop me from cracking the case.

Then—dammit!—that front door opened, and I knew something else.

I knew the woman who stood in the doorway.

Crap! Crap! Crap!

"You must be D, Elizabeth's mother," she said extending a friendly hand. "I'm the housekeeper, Caryn."

Yes, of course she was. Caryn Summers.

Her smile was wide and genuine. Unfaltering. Her eyes didn't flare or flicker with recognition as we shook hands. Not yet. It had been a lot of years since we'd seen each other…

Marport City is a good-sized city—big enough, generally, to provide anonymity for someone like me. And naturally, since I grew up here, I know it like the back of my hand. I know every street, every dive, all the rough hangouts. Yep, I had been a wild child. Truth be told, I still was. I can blend in, or hide out in, any part of town.

But every once in a while, the past catches up to me.

Like right then.

Caryn Summers and I had gone to high school together. Both of us had been in Mr. Mulligan's home room class in our junior year. Briefly. She hadn't lasted at Marport City Central High.

She was smart, I recalled. But Caryn's anxiety in high school had been almost palpable. And very sad. She looked scared shitless all the time. Totally out of place. I have no doubt she'd spent her days counting down the minutes until the bell rang at three thirty.

Then one day just before Christmas, Caryn's anxiety hadn't been so palpable. Not even close. She'd laughed with the cool kids and joked with the assholes and sat back in the cafeteria looking so relaxed. Nor had she been a bundle of teenage nerves and angst the next day. Or the following few days after that. Even back then I'd been nosy. My younger sister was concerned. So Peaches Marie and I started snooping around. We asked some questions—listened to the gossip. And we soon learned the reason for Caryn's more relaxed state of being.

Caryn turned to Mrs. P. "And you must be—?"

"Call me, Nanny Jane. That's what everyone calls me. I'm this one's mother," she said, jerking her thumb toward me.

"I'm so pleased to meet you, Nanny Jane. Elizabeth has spoken so highly of you."

"I bet she has."

Caryn's smile turned even friendlier as she took Dylan's outstretched hand. "My, but you've got a strong grip."

"Magnus Quinn," Dylan said, and Caryn's free hand flitted to her chest in a flustered way as his grip on her fingers lingered.

Dylan's eyes seemed to warm as he took in this stylish and pretty age-mate of mine. Too warm? Dammit. I hated to wonder if he had a thing for older women in general. Um, I mean *older* compared to him, not *older* as in...old, er.

I thought I was the only one.

Playing the part, Dix, I reminded myself. He's just playing the part. In full-blown, mustachioed gigolo mode.

Fine. But if he started flashing those socks…

A scream—loud and shrill and panicked—jerked me out of my ruminations. The shriek was followed immediately by the sound of something—or someone—hitting the floor with a thump.

"Dear God!" Caryn pulled her hand free of Dylan's. "What on earth was that?"

"It's an axe murderer!" Mrs. P shouted, shoving me toward

the door.

I was pretty sure it wasn't an axe murderer, but I *did* start running—full tilt into the house, following the cries for help. With Dylan right behind me, we raced through an immaculate room, down a wide corridor, and ended up in what could only be Hugh's study.

"Don't hurt him!" That cry came loud and clear from Caryn, who arrived right behind Dylan and me.

Elizabeth, from her unique position—or not so unique position, considering it was Elizabeth Bee—echoed the don't-hurt-him sentiment in a muffled and out-of-breath way, like someone with a heavy weight on her chest.

Why? Because she had a heavy weight on her chest. To wit, her husband.

My razor-sharp PI mind took in the scene in an instant. Dark liquid spreading out on the hardwood floor. A large and miraculously unbroken Oktoberfest mug lay upturned and empty. Crackers, cheese, and tiny pickles were scattered on the polished hardwood floor. One of the room's many small decorative rugs was scrunched aside. It was, of course, the only rug askew in the place. That had to be the source of the mishap, scream, and subsequent cries for help.

Hugh had slipped and fallen, spilling the drink and food. But Elizabeth, ever the doting wife, had broken his fall. Literally. No way was she allowing her sugar daddy husband to hit the deck.

Now Hugh looked like he was doing some sort of yoga maneuver. My sister Peaches Marie and her partner are big-time into yoga. Last time they'd visited, both women had tried to get me to contort myself into a few of those positions. Something had cracked inside, I swear.

What Hugh was currently doing looked like a modified downward facing dog. Er, sorta. More than forming an arch himself, he was arching over Elizabeth's ample chest, balancing on those mountains of love.

Elizabeth was flat on her back on the gleaming hardwood

floor, arms out and legs splayed as if she was trying to make a snow angel on the wood there. Then the thought hit me: I'd just captured "Elizabeth" and "angel" in the same thought! I felt like laughing right out loud.

"Don't just stand there laughing, *Mother*," Elizabeth puffed. "Help your son-in-law get up."

"Let me," Dylan said. "I've taken a little first aid."

That was true, he had. Well, actually, it was more than a *little* first aid. The boy had some serious skills. Besides, with his six-foot-four frame, he could easily help the older gentleman to his feet, brittle bones and all, without anything snapping out of place.

Caryn chewed her nails anxiously. "Oh, please be careful."

Dylan and I each grabbed an elbow. Hugh's old dog growled low in his throat. Not aggressively as much as warningly.

"Easy, Humphrey," Caryn soothed. "Come here, good dog." She put on that voice—the unmistakable, unfakeable dog-lover's voice.

The dog went to her. Caryn hooked a hand around his collar. Humphrey looked up at her worriedly. "Good boy, Humphrey. He'll be okay."

With Dylan on one side of Hugh and me on the other, we got him back on his feet. And we didn't let go of those smoking jacket-wrapped arms until his old butt was on the sofa. He sat back with a sigh of relief. Dylan and I stepped back, and he gave us an appreciative smile.

Ah, but the most relieved person in the room just then was easily Elizabeth Bee-Drammen.

"Oh, Hugh-Bear!"

Elizabeth had jumped up when we'd lifted Hugh from on top of her. Now that he was sitting safely on the sofa, she ran over to him. Dylan and I took another step back. Translation: we got the hell out of the way before she plowed us over.

"Are you okay, Hugh?" Caryn asked.

"Fine, Caryn, dear. Nothing to worry about."

I expected Elizabeth to throw her arms around Hugh-Bear, but she didn't. Not right away, at least. But she did start checking him out. "Are you sure you're okay?" With one hand on his shoulders, she stared into his eyes.

"How many fingers am I holding up?" she asked.

"Four," I answered.

"Oh for God's sake, not you, Mother!"

"Elizabeth," Hugh said, his tone gentle but assertive. "I'm fine."

Elizabeth patted her way down the rest of him. "Nothing broken? Nothing hurts?" She checked him out from ankle to neck like she was in charge of airport security. Except it wasn't quite so groping.

Wringing her hands, Caryn asked, "Should I call an ambulance?"

"Yes," Elizabeth said, turning to her. "I think we'd better–"

Doing his best to stifle a groan, Hugh cringed as he sat up straight. "I just slipped on that darn rug. Nobody's calling an ambulance."

"Are you sure?" Elizabeth did one more visual scan as she sat down beside him. "Oh, if anything ever happened to you…"

Hugh gave Elizabeth a reassuring pat on the hand. "Nothing's going to happen to me for a good many years, Elizabeth." He looked to his housekeeper. "Caryn, you can let Humphrey go. Poor thing must be terrified."

Caryn released her grip on the dog's collar, and the whining mongrel trotted straight to his master. With a comforting hand on the dog's over-sized furry head, Hugh gave Humphrey the same reassurance he'd given his wife.

All was well. So I started scoping out the place.

The study was beyond immaculate. And orderly. And kind of eclectic.

With my quick perusal, I ascertained this: Every piece of furniture was pulled the same distance from the wall. There were a few paintings on the walls in there too, all hung at the same height. The books were neatly—evenly—aligned on the oak shelving, and I would wager that there were more than a few collectors' editions among the old tomes.

From the pens and pads on the mahogany desk to the fall of the lace sheers over the patio doors, everything was orderly. Almost everything.

There was also evidence of the fire. Just above the sofa, two narrow shelves of books were missing. Well, the shelves themselves were still there, but the books had been carted off. They'd probably been damaged beyond repair by smoke and fire extinguisher chemicals, if not by flame. The damage was evident on the shelves in the form of black charring.

How the hell could a fire have started there?

Obviously assured that his master was all right, Humphrey headed for the spilled munchies, wolfed them down, and made a bee-line for the ale. He sniffed it and then swung his head around to Hugh.

"Enjoy," Hugh said dryly.

Humphrey started lapping up the beer.

"Shall I get you another?" Elizabeth said.

"I can get it, Elizabeth," Caryn said.

Hugh looked down at his watch—a thick, clunky old model—and shook his head. "Thank you, but no. Time's past. And," he looked again at Dylan and me, "I see we have company. Company which I now have to thank for their assistance."

"Think nothing of it," Dylan said. "Glad to help."

Hugh nodded to Dylan and turned to me. "You must be Elizabeth's mother." Suddenly, he hesitated. His eyes narrowed.

I was almost sure that recognition was dawning. Yes, I am that unforgettable.

So I did what any PI in my shoes would do. I upped my disguise. Dug a little deeper under cover. Yes, I threw back my shoulders and thrust out my well-padded chest. Well, Elizabeth *had* said that her husband was a boob man…

Tada!

I was just about to throw in jazz hands when Hugh turned that quizzical look to his wife. "Did you hear something?"

Elizabeth held perfectly still, listening. Then she rolled her eyes. "Oh no."

I heard it too, growing ever louder—the stomping down the hall toward the study.

"What the devil's going on in here?" Tammy Drammen practically bowled poor Caryn over as she thundered into the room. She did not look happy.

Her husband, Allen, followed a couple of seconds later, carrying a martini replete with no less than three olives. Though he held the glass high, it looked as if he was dangling it. Like it was an accessory, a prop to go along with the ascot and smoking jacket he wore. Amazing how that type of jacket could look so dapper on an older man like Hugh and so stupid on a...well, Allen Boyden.

Tammy took in the situation with snapping eyes. The spill the dog was still slurping up, a rattled Elizabeth sitting beside Hugh. Caryn standing quietly. Then Tammy's eyes settled on me, and those eyes kept right on snapping. So did her tongue.

"Does your back hurt?" she asked me.

Probably a fair question, given my chest-extending pose, but one of those potential jazz hands still wanted to smack her.

I let my shoulders slide back into their normal posture. Oh, and I assumed my D Bee cougar mode.

"My back can be a little twitchy," I drawled. "But not for long. You know what they say about sex curing a bad back. I'm Elizabeth's mother." I put a proprietary hand on Dylan's arm. "This is my back doctor, Magnus Quinn."

Dylan wrapped an arm around me, lowered his hand, and playfully slapped my butt. I tee-heed and snuggled in closer. Under normal—and definitely private—circumstances, Dylan Foreman's hand on my derriere was a thrill. However, these were not normal circumstances.

I'm not one for PDA at the best of times, but while such a

display wouldn't be in Dix Dodd's repertoire, I imagined it would be in D Bee's.

"Yes," I said. "I've hardly had a twitch since Magnus came along. Though I do seem to be feeling a bit of an ache tonight..."

Tammy didn't say a word, but I could read the distaste on her face.

"Gosh, Tammy darling," Allen said. "If sex is good for the back, it's amazing you can even stand upright. What's it been for us...six, seven years? Oh, or maybe that's just for me."

What an asshole.

Okay, I get it. I've been a PI long enough to know the sex life between married couples often wanes a few years post-honeymoon. I mean, life gets busy, jobs get stressful, kids come along, the networks start rerunning *Murder She Wrote* at bedtime...or eight o'clock, as some people call it. And do not get me started on *Dancing with the Stars*! But come on, most people aren't ready to shout that news in public or even to voice their suspicions out loud. No, most people hire me instead to see if their spouses are getting it somewhere else.

"Tammy, Allen, please. This isn't the time for a fight," Hugh admonished. "Elizabeth's family's here."

Tammy shot—and I mean, shot—Allen a scathing look. "Are you still here?" she said, articulating every word clearly.

I had a feeling she didn't mean just the room.

Allen's smile didn't disappear, but it definitely lost that smarmy edge. And it was Allen who lost the ensuing stare-down between him and his wife. Unfortunately, after that losing blink, his eyes turned to me.

"Don't mind my wife. She's a bit of a...stuffed shirt, shall we say. But not in that good way..."

Oh God, he started to eyeball my literally stuffed shirt.

I wanted to smack him too but restrained myself. Dammit, would these hands never dance again?

Stay in the role, D.

"Well, hello there," I said.

Allen saluted me with a sip of his martini. God, the guy was like a blast from the sixties. A British sixties, except just not that hot. He stood there in a plum-colored velvet smoking jacket, with his mop-top haircut which was obviously dyed that perfectly even chestnut brown. His eyes never left mine as he sipped the martini again. Loudly. Oh crap, *suggestively*. He waggled his bushy eyebrows.

This was just too weird. The knob was flirting with me! Right in front of his wife and my...um...back doctor.

"What happened in here?" Tammy snapped at Elizabeth, drawing our attention.

"My husband slipped," Elizabeth answered. "I saw him start to go, and I broke his fall before he hit the floor. My mother and Magnus helped him up. He's fine, Tammy."

"Daddy never slipped before you came here, Elizabeth." Tammy's manicured nails disappeared into tight fists.

Elizabeth's chin jutted out as she grabbed Hugh's hand. "Well, good thing I was here to help him now, wasn't it, Tams?"

"Tams? I told you never to call me that."

Whoa, was that the same Tammy Drammen from the wedding? The one who'd been so happy to stand up with her father and Elizabeth? Did I slip into the wrong wedding or something? That's only kind of rhetorical...I've done it before.

Whatever had happened between those two?

Allen raised his glass again, winked at me, and chuckled. "Welcome to the Drammen family meet-and-greet. Someone always ends up on the floor but usually not literally."

"Oh, shut up!" Tammy and Elizabeth hissed at him in unison.

"How many of those have you had, Allen?" Hugh asked, gesturing to the drink in his son-in-law's hand.

"Counting is for juniors." He tossed it back like an old pro. But grimaced like an amateur as it went down. "Juniors and obsessive old men."

Dylan and I exchanged a glance. Oh boy, all hell was about

to break loose. And there we were in the middle of it. Poor Humphrey was whining again and not just because the ale was gone. His big, brown, worried dog eyes moved back and forth between the angry parties.

Then came the unmistakable sound of a toilet flushing across the hall. Twice.

Tammy turned to Caryn. "Shouldn't the day staff be gone by now?"

"They are," Caryn confirmed. "Oh, it must be—"

"What did I miss?" Tucking her shirt in, Mrs. P, aka Nanny Jane, joined us in the study. "I heard some yelling."

Tammy gave her a confused look. "And you are…?"

"Nanny Jane," Mrs. P extended her hand. "How do you do?"

It was enough to jog Tammy's memory. "Of course," she grated, "the grandmother. It just keeps getting merrier." She left Mrs. P's hand hanging there.

And that settled it: I did not like this woman.

Okay, it was one thing to be snide to me. Fine. I could handle it. Likewise, Dylan. He is a big boy. But that's not important right now. (I mean, would he have given me a plastic prick if he wasn't?) However, I should add—he could handle himself too.

But when Tams started on Mrs. P, I could feel the fine hairs elevating on my neck. Feel my temperature rising. I was pissed. Not that Mrs. Presley was defenseless or frail. But she was Mrs. P.

"Didn't you hear my mother?" I grated. "She said *how do you do?*" I would not blow my cover, would not blow the case. But I absolutely sure as hell would not stand for anyone being rude to Mrs. P like that.

Tammy huffed but answered. "I'm fine." Then she shook her head and took another deep breath, a calming one, it seemed. "I'm sorry. I seem to have misplaced my manners. Nice to meet you, Jane."

"Call me Nanny Jane," Mrs. P said.

No way would Tammy would call her that, but at least she knew enough to grab Mrs. P's hand for a quick shake.

I glanced over at Elizabeth to see that she had paled as this exchange had gone on. Her eyes grew wider, and a sheen of sweat broke out on her forehead. She gave me a WTF kind of look, and I knew just what she was thinking. *This is the only sweet little old lady you could dig up?*

After sliding her smile past Tammy, Nanny Jane spotted Elizabeth on the couch beside Hugh. "Oh, my little Boo-Boo," she screeched. "Come say hi to your old Nanny Jane. Give your Nanny a hug."

Mrs. Presley's purse rattled off her arm and thudded to the floor as she dropped it. She opened her arms wide for that long-overdue embrace.

"All right." Elizabeth stood. She walked to her "grandmother" with a tight smile on her face. "I've missed you, Nanny Ja—Jesus!"

"I missed you more!" Mrs. P threw her arms around Elizabeth and gave her a boa constrictor squeeze. Whereas Mrs. P is on the short side and Elizabeth definitely isn't, Elizabeth had to bend down into the embrace. Mrs. P kissed her on the cheek and held her tightly. She rocked her shoulders back and forth. Elizabeth, wearing heels, pivoted on them precariously with every overdone left-right pull.

"My goodness," Mrs. P said, "the stories I could tell you all about this one! This little rascal—the mischief she used to get herself into."

"Do tell," Allen said.

"Why, I think I will." Mrs. P finally released her grip on Elizabeth.

Well, Elizabeth had said she'd needed a grandmother. She didn't say it couldn't be the grandmother from hell.

CHAPTER 4

MRS. P/NANNY Jane was having a wonderful time. She coaxed and persuaded until her dear "granddaughter" finally agreed to sing "I'm a Little Teapot" just like she used to do back home. While tap dancing. Then of course Mrs. P started with the Elizabeth stories, all completely embarrassing and one hundred percent made up.

There wasn't a single thing Elizabeth could do to stop it. Not without blowing our cover.

"Oh, and don't even get me started on that time Elizabeth ate that strawberry shortcake just before cheerleading practice," Mrs. P said. "Remember that, my little Boo-Boo? She gave Elizabeth a sharp...um, affectionate aren't-you-cute pinch on the cheek. "You couldn't get off that field fast enough. And the bathrooms were so far away!"

"Actually, Nanny Jane," she said. "I think you must be mistaken. I don't remember that at all."

"Oh, I remember it," I said.

Elizabeth shot me an evil look.

What? I was just working the character! Hee hee hee.

It was Caryn who finally put the civility back into the situation. Or at least tried to.

"Why don't we all go into the parlor and get more comfortable?" she said.

"And get another drink." Allen saluted with his glass again. That time in Caryn's direction. "I'm thinking a highball."

"Of course, Allen," Caryn answered brightly.

She was first to leave the room.

Humphrey stayed behind. Having no interest in the Elizabeth stories, the old dog retired to his mat by the patio doors. He plunked down and by all appearances was out like a light. Probably the beer didn't hurt.

Jealous much? Why yes, actually. And not just because of the beer. (I love beer!) No, I didn't envy the dog his rabbit-chasing dreams, but I did envy that out-like-a-light sleep. Not to mention Humphrey's certitude that he'd stay put during his nap, give or take a few whimpers and leg quivers/twitches. No flailing around. No banging into things.

It's fine when I'm home and increasingly fine when I sleep over at Dylan's place. But honestly, I am paranoid about my sleep disorder. I really didn't want to start thrashing around and breaking furniture in the place. But even without any furniture breakage, my thumping around can get loud. Maybe I should have mentioned to Elizabeth that I can be a noisy sleeper. If I'd thought to forewarn her, she could have put me in an isolated bedroom, preferably one without valuable antiques. But I really don't like a lot of people knowing my private business.

But how I do love to know theirs…

"Follow me," Tammy said.

"Well, that shouldn't be hard, the way you clomp around like that," Allen interjected.

"Allen, don't start!"

Don't start? I doubted those two ever stopped!

"Wait up, Tammy!" Mrs. P said. "I was thinking...they

must have some really high-stakes bingo games in this neighborhood. Do you like bingo?"

"Bingo?" Tammy looked truly flustered. "I've never played."

"I doubt there are any bingo halls around here, Nanny Jane," Dylan said.

She nodded. "That's too bad." Mrs. Presley grabbed up her purse and followed Tammy and Allen out of the room.

Yes, Mrs. P had packed her bingo dabbers. I saw them when she'd clunked down her purse to give Elizabeth that open-armed greeting. And it was a pretty safe bet there was at least one lucky, pink-haired troll doll biding its time in her suitcase right now, ready to jump out and kill us! Sorry, I meant jump out and call up the bingo gods.

Dolls just creep me out. Dolls and chalk dust. Always have. And yes, I'd freakin' hated kindergarten.

"Need help getting up, Hugh-Bear?" Elizabeth asked.

"If you wouldn't mind, my dear."

With Dylan on one side and Elizabeth on the other, they eased Hugh to his feet. He looked at me and smiled. "Wonderful to having caring, young hands around, isn't it? Aren't we the lucky ones, D? To have companions who are so much younger than we are?" He winked at me to punctuate the statement. Or was it to mark our geriatric kinship?

Half my age plus nine! I wanted to shout, but I couldn't very well do that. Sometimes it sucks to stay in character. I smiled at Hugh and nodded. Ground my teeth together and stole a look at Dylan.

Where others wouldn't even notice, I saw that stiffening in his demeanor with Hugh's remark.

"Not so much younger with D and me, Hugh," Dylan said. "Just right. I'm exactly half her age plus—"

Dylan shut up quickly.

Hugh chuckled. "You've done the math, I see."

Dylan's eyes shot to me. Then quickly shot away.

Dammit! He *had* done the math. Checked out that half-your-age-plus thing that I was so iron-fistedly clinging to. Should it bother me that he had? Hell yes, it should. Because I now knew the age gap between us was more of a concern for him than he was letting on.

Dylan let go of Hugh as soon as he was steady on his feet, but Elizabeth stayed linked to his arm. Slowly, they left the study.

As I was about to exit around him, Dylan grabbed my hand and gave it a reassuring squeeze. "All good, Dix?" he whispered sexily. Nice and slow and low.

"Pardon me?"

"All good?"

"What?" I raised my voice.

"I SAID—"

"Sorry, young whippersnapper. You'll have to speak up. You know, my being so much older."

"Ah, having trouble hearing, are we?" He hauled me up against him in a move fit for the role he was playing. With his mouth at my ear, he said, "Can you hear me now, D?"

I shivered as his warm breath stirred the hair at my neck. "Um...yes. I can hear you much better."

"Are you sure? Maybe you should try reading my lips."

"But I don't lip read."

"Sure you do." He tipped up my chin and kissed me. And yes, yes, I was getting the message.

"Are you two coming?" Elizabeth called from the hallway.

Dammit, we'd just got started!

Grinning at me, Dylan took my hand, and we went out to join the others.

I'd already seen that part of the house when we'd hightailed it to the study, but as we walked along at Hugh Drammen's leisurely pace, I got a much better look at things. And I came to this conclusion: I'd never sleep.

Yikes. What if I damaged one of those Tiffany lamps or a piece of expensive furniture? They must be worth a fortune. And oh, God, many of the rooms had stained-glass windows that were no doubt custom crafted.

I should have been more specific about what *expenses* on this job might entail.

We'd reached the parlor, which was beyond beautiful, not to mention luxurious, elegant, and stupidly big. But it was...cold. Not in a throw-another-log-on-the-fire way. Not even a find-yourself-a-strapping-lumberjack-to-make-love-by-the-woodstove-on-a-bear-skin-rug way.

I stared up at the high ceiling with its arched wooden beams. The stately room was furnished with solid furniture, and I'd have bet my bottom dollar most of it was antique (thank you, *Antiques Roadshow*). The chandeliers were bright and elegant. The room really should have felt welcoming and gracious, but somehow it had an emotional coolness to it.

Cool or not, I found myself coveting some of the pieces. That chandelier, for instance or those awesome floor-to-ceiling drapery panels.

Don't get me wrong, I'm okay with my place. More than okay with it. I love my cozy little space. But those things were...nice.

I did a little mental arithmetic. The Drammen mansion had to be worth at least five or six million. The pieces in this room alone probably added up to a hundred large.

Jesus, caffeine, and toothpicks! If my room was anything like this, I definitely would not sleep.

Elizabeth had talked about two million dollars to be bequeathed to her. Would this beautiful home fall in or out of her grasp if something were to happen to Hugh? Out, I guessed.

"'Lo there."

Okay, I pride myself on being observant, but honestly the man sitting so still and unassuming at the back of the room had completely escaped my notice. Not even kidding.

Morris Drammen. He sat leaning forward, knees apart, hands together. He nodded an acknowledgement to us all. Leaned back, crossed his legs, and then uncrossed them.

I felt so sorry for the guy. He'd looked out of place at the wedding. But you'd think, still being there in Casa Drammen, he'd have gotten over that, at least to some extent. But Morris Drammen, in his Wal-Mart jeans, flannel shirt in a muted plaid, and fur-trimmed moccasins on his feet, looked completely out of place. The proverbial FUD in the dildo drawer.

FUD in the dildo drawer?

Wow, a metaphor! I was just about to tell everyone when Hugh spoke up.

"Please have a seat."

I sat on a long rose-patterned sofa. Sat? More like sank into it. It was the softest, plushest, most comfortable thing my butt had ever landed in. Dylan gave a little sigh as he sank down beside me. I glanced at him, trying to figure out if that was a this-feels-nice reaction or a my-boy-parts-are-getting-squished-in-all-this-plushness kind of thing.

He gave me a smile that was more of a grimace, so probably the latter.

Mrs. P/Nanny Jane sat down close on the other side of Dylan. She patted her hand on the empty cushion to her left. "Boo-Boo, come sit beside your Nanny. I just want to squeeze you so much."

"Oh, I always sit with my husband, Nanny Jane," she answered. "You always told me when I found my true love to keep him close. Don't you remember, dear?"

Well played, Boo-Boo Bee. Well played.

Yes, I was on the case, but that didn't stop me from enjoying the contest between those two.

Mrs. P's grin did not slip a fraction. "Oh yes, now I remember. That bit of advice was right up there with 'be sure to wear clean underwear in case you're in an accident'. Remember, Boo-Boo? But you thought it was 'be sure to wear clean underwear and then have an accident'. Damn those strawberries." She turned to Hugh. "But the home team won by a touchdown. That's the important thing."

Elizabeth's lips thinned.

Hugh settled himself in a chair near the room's grand fireplace, and Elizabeth sat with great relief in a smaller but matching chair right beside him. They held hands briefly and smiled at each other.

"That used to be Mother's chair," Tammy said tightly.

"I know, Tammy," Elizabeth said. "So you've said. Quite a few times actually. But now it's my place beside your father."

With a huff, Tammy sat on a love seat by the bar. She sat very close to one end, leaving plenty of room, but...

Did I mention it was a long couch I'd sat down on?

Allen squeezed in beside me, regardless of Dylan occupying the space on the other side. I smiled at him; he smiled back. I giggled, as he tapped my knee with his martini glass.

In character. Absolutely, I was in full floozy character. Flirtatious, man-crazy D Bee me (God, there must be a limerick in the making here). As much as Allen Boyden repulsed Dix Dodd, I had to play my role.

So I giggled all the more; I batted my eyelashes. Oh, by the way, I suck at batting my eyelashes. Seriously, suck at it.

"Why are your eyes doing that?" Allen asked. He squinted as he looked at me closely. "Are you having a seizure?"

Tammy sat up. "A seizure?"

"Oh that," Mrs. P said helpfully. "It's just a twitch. A nervous thing. That happens whenever she gets too excited."

Gee, thanks, Nanny Jane.

"I've heard of things like that—twitches and the like."

That conversational gem—spoken like someone who didn't know what to say but who figured he should say something—was contributed by Morris. Clearly small talk was not one of his strengths. In fact, it was probably fair to say it agonized him. It didn't take my awesome PI skills to see that he had some serious social anxiety going on.

Cheeks flaming, Morris turned away, studying the landscape painting to his right and no doubt wishing he could melt right into it.

Yeah, well I wouldn't have minded that myself.

Unfortunately, Allen had taken Mrs. P's comment about that whole twitch-arousal thing as encouragement. He sidled his butt a little closer on the couch.

Or rather, tried to.

"Dude," Dylan said. "The lady's with me."

I think what Dylan had meant to say was that the *hot, foxy lady* was with him, but I'd let it slide this time.

"It's cool, Magnus," Allen said. "Just being friendly, is all."

"Then I suggest you not be so friendly."

Contrary to the *I suggest* part of Dylan's comment, it was more than a suggestion. Allen was smart enough to recognize that and got up to stand beside a statue of his wife.

Oh wait, that *was* his wife. She'd jumped from the loveseat when Allen had called "seizure" and was standing now by the bar. Stone cold with anger. Allen winked at me.

I winked back, because that's what D would do.

"Oh yeah," Morris said. "That's some sort of seizure, all right."

Did I mention I suck at winking also?

Oh, and *yuck*. I'd hated winking at that jerk. Any man who would stand there in front of his wife and flirt like that with another woman was a total dick. But I wanted to stay on Allen's good side. Perhaps he could be a resource during the investigation. Tammy, on the other hand, didn't seem likely to help, so there was no point trying to ally myself with her. But Allen…

I laughed out loud as if Allen was the funniest thing. Then I laughed and laughed some more. I jiggled as I giggled.

"Careful, Mother," Elizabeth said. "You don't want to pee yourself."

Mrs. P reached across Dylan to pat my knee. "Yes, dear. We had that whole pelvic floor talk for a reason. Have you been doing your Kegels?"

Dylan jumped to my defense. "She sure has. She's on her back with her feet in those stirrups all the time. Doing all those contortions, groaning about what terrible torture it is. But she's committed to firming up."

What the hell? "No, Dylan," I said evenly. "That's *pilates*."

"Oh, sorry. Pilates, Kegels. What's the difference?"

"Well, for starters, it looks nothing like pilates, or exercise of any kind, for that matter. In fact, you have to be careful *not* to flex your abdomen or butt or thighs. With Kegels, you just sort of…squeeze and hold"

Elizabeth frowned. "Squeeze and hold *what*?"

She was kidding, right?

"I think we all could use a drink," Caryn said brightly.

For a moment, I felt relief not to be explaining Kegels to a woman too young to have to worry about what might happen if she sneezed, but that turned to a very real uneasiness. We could *all* use a drink? *Caryn*?

"Wine," Tammy said. "Lots and lots of wine."

So much for guests first. Then again, the quicker we liquored Tammy up, the quicker she might loosen up. Loose lips and all that.

Caryn opened the liquor cabinet and set to work. First up? Red wine for Tammy. I love red wine myself, and I recognized that particular Cabernet Sauvignon as being out of my price range, at least for ordinary consumption. Tammy swirled it in the big balloon glass, and I expected her to sip it appreciatively. Instead, she raised the glass to her lips and downed half of it.

Sacrilege!

I turned my attention back to Caryn, who was pouring a couple of fingers of Glenfiddich, neat, for Elizabeth. Next up was a Diet Coke for Hugh, no ice. She reached for a martini glass, but Allen stopped her.

"I'll get mine, Caryn."

"What would you like, Nanny Jane?"

"I'd love a Baileys, if you have it."

Hugh looked toward Caryn, who nodded and turned back to the bar.

"What about you, D? Magnus?"

"I'd love some of that red wine," I said.

"Beer for me," Dylan said. "Any kind."

Allen bellied up to the bar, literally. At first, I couldn't figure if he was leaning close for balance or moving in to hump that piece of mahogany furniture. Ah, wish I were kidding on that latter thing. In this line of work, I've seen a lot. People have some strange fetishes. But enough about me.

While idle chatter drifted around me—Mrs. P must have written a freakin' notebook full of Elizabeth Boo-Boo stories—I watched Allen and Caryn standing there together, working in such close proximity. Glasses tinkling. Feet bumping. Yeah. All his doing. He was too close.

Caryn, who clearly didn't like the proximity to Allen, managed to inch away without drawing attention.

Hugh cleared his throat loudly. "Allen, why don't you get out of the way while Caryn pours drinks for our guests?"

Whoops, guess someone else had noticed.

Allen said nothing, but he did step back, fresh martini in hand.

Caryn handed me my glass of wine. As she looked at me, Caryn Summers stopped cold. "You look familiar, D. Have we met?"

Crap!

"Ever been to—?"

"Louisville, Kentucky." Elizabeth interjected quickly before I could say another word. So that's where she'd told the Drammens she hailed from.

Truth?

Nope. At least not judging by the fleeting look in Elizabeth's eyes as we glanced at each other.

"Louisville, Kentucky?" Caryn shook her head. "No, I've never been much out of Marport City."

"Lucky for us," Hugh said. "Caryn's been with us for many

years."

Caryn turned to Morris, who was clutching a Molson Canadian. "Another for you?"

He shook his head. "I'm fine."

Everyone else having been served, I watched Caryn place a new glass on the bar top. Unlike the others, this glass was smoky green. It looked like it had come straight out of the seventies. One by one, Caryn counted out four ice cubes from the ice bucket and dropped them into the glass. She grabbed a Diet Coke, tapped the tab three times with her fingernail, and snapped it open.

Diet Coke, huh? Would she pour a shot into it?

No. In fact, after she took her first drink, she didn't even stick around.

"I'm going to clean up the mess in the study, Hugh," she said.

Tammy frowned. "Can't it wait? Lois or Glori—"

"Oh, it won't take long," Caryn said, half turning as she walked. "I'll just—"

The sentence ended on a groan. Caryn's hand shot to her lower back.

"Is your back bothering you, dear?" Hugh asked.

Caryn shook her head. "I'm fine. It's nothing." She straightened, smiled, and walked out of the room quickly.

"Is she okay?" Dylan asked.

It was Tammy who answered. "She's had a bad back for a while, but she really aggravated in November. She's seen an orthopedic surgeon—a friend of mine. He squeezed her in as a favor. He thinks he can help her surgically, so now she's waiting for it to be scheduled."

"How did she hurt it?" I asked.

Silence.

"Well don't everyone talk at once," Mrs. P said.

"It was just one of those things, Nanny Jane," Allen offered. "Just a bad twist...making a bed or something." He tossed back his drink.

Making a bed or something? Bullshit.

Ah, the shifting eyes. Whatever had happened to Caryn was a lip-sealed secret.

Morris stood suddenly. "Well, thanks for the drink." As if realizing the glass of Molson was still in his hand—untouched—he tipped the glass up and downed it in a couple of swallows. Impressive. It looked like Morris Drammen was a man who'd shot-gunned a few beers in his day.

"Leaving so soon, man?" Dylan said.

He nodded. "Yeah, busy day tomorrow. Well, good night." A moment later he was out the door.

Tammy, apparently deciding to be civil now, explained, "Morris spends almost all his time in the workshop out back of the main house. He's brilliant with antique repair, and we're getting him to restore some family treasures. Finally. My mother loved old things. She acquired quite a collection. We're incorporating some of those pieces into the house as Morris fixes them." She pointed to an elegant straight-back chair in the corner.

"That's lovely." Mrs. P handed me her Baileys and went over to examine it. She ran a hand along the chair's intricately carved back.

"Morris is now working on a lovely Queen Anne desk," Tammy said. "For me."

"Don't you mean for me?" Elizabeth said. "It's going in my study."

Any civility that may have been trying to breathe in the room flew up the chimney. Like, really fast.

"Your father said I could fix my study up any way I wanted. That was his gift to me," Elizabeth said. "I want that Queen Anne desk. That's the one thing you said you didn't mind me having."

"I changed my mind."

"You can't just do that!"

Allen, who seemed to have decided that it was the perfect time to be even more of an asshole, said, "Why don't you saw it in half, like they did with that baby in the Bible? Or was that from Shakespeare?"

Oh God, was the guy a total idiot?

"Don't be an idiot," Elizabeth said.

With that, Allen was in on the argument too. Voices rose. Insults were traded.

Wow… that was how they comported themselves when they had company?

I felt eyes on me and turned to find Hugh watching me. He sighed deeply, deflated in the chair. Then he tipped his drink in salute. "Welcome to the family, Dix Dodd."

Hugh gave "Magnus" a similar Diet Coke salute and winked at him.

But despite my admiration of Hugh's talented eyelids (nobody would ask *him* what was wrong with his eye), panic started to crawl its way in.

He'd called me Dix Dodd! He knew.

CHAPTER 5

WAS IT HOT in there or was that just me? And yeah, that whole *just me* scenario was a real possibility.

But, crap! Hugh knew!

Despite Elizabeth's reassurances that he only had eyes for certain assets—which I'm beginning to believe was more wishful thinking on her part than anything else—her husband had definitely pegged Dylan and me from the Cuddle Club.

But he continued to smile. That is, until he turned his attention once more to the bickering in front of him.

I watched the back and forth. So did Dylan and Mrs. Presley.

Tammy was going on about maternal affection. Elizabeth was asserting her place as the new Mrs. Drammen. Allen was being a dick. Seriously. At that point, he wasn't even speaking anymore, but he just had that total dick vibe.

That went on for a few minutes, until Hugh finally said, "My dears, you're upsetting Humphrey."

Humphrey was still down the hall, no doubt sleeping off the Guinness. But that had to mean something significant in Drammen-speak, because the argument silenced at once.

And believe it or not, not ten seconds after that, near

normal conversation ensued.

Soon Caryn came back into the parlor smelling like that pine-fresh scent. I thought she'd been gone an inordinate amount of time for such a small task as cleaning up after Humphrey, but hey, what do I know about such things? Okay, yes, I do clean. Just...quickly. Infrequently. Frankly, the whole idea of having a dog around to lap up spills was looking pretty damned attractive.

Caryn offered another round of drinks. Everyone declined. That signaled the party was over. Which was fine with me. I wasn't getting anywhere here.

It was apparently fine with everyone. They scattered without another word to one another and barely a nod to Dylan, Mrs. P, and me.

Caryn sighed relief. She smiled. "I'll show you to your rooms."

"Stairs or elevator?" Caryn asked. Then she quickly added, "Actually, do you mind if we take the elevator?"

"Elevator's fine," I answered quickly. And not just out of consideration for Caryn and her bad back. Not that I was opposed to stairs and getting a little bit of cardio, but I'd never been in a house with an elevator before. I was kind of curious.

"Almost forgot," Dylan said suddenly. "I'll go get the bags."

Of course! We'd left them on the step when we'd raced into the house.

"Taken care of." Caryn pushed the elevator call button. "They're already up in your rooms."

"You didn't carry them, did you?" Mrs. P asked.

"No, I didn't. Morris must have gotten them."

"That was good of him," I said. "Morris seems very handy around here, don't you think?"

Emphasis on the *handy*. Yes, I was searching for gossip. A

titter. A tee hee. A hint of anything...

"Very handy." Caryn answered without a flicker of emotion.

"I'm sure Elizabeth finds him particularly handy." Hint, hint...I all but elbowed her in the ribs.

"We all do."

Again, nothing. Not a conspiratorial lowering of voice or provocative lift of eyebrow, despite my let's-share-a-secret wink.

"You really should get that eye looked at," she said.

Beside me, Dylan laughed.

We took the elevator up to the second floor. I thought it would be tight with the four of us, but it was quite spacious. It lulled more than zipped its way up and stopped with a definite little bounce. As the doors whispered open, I caught a glimpse of Hugh and Elizabeth slipping into the room at the far end of the hall.

Caryn stopped our party at the first door on the left. "Magnus, this is your room." She opened the door.

"Thank you, Caryn, and good night." Dylan moved past her. "Night, Nanny Jane. You too, sweet cheeks. Sweet dreams."

Yeah. He meant me. *Blech.* Pet names.

"Sleep well, honey," I answered. "Try not to stay up too late reading."

He acknowledged me with a nod. But not just any old nod—he'd definitely gotten my drift.

Reading. Yes, he'd meet me in the study later on.

Caryn stopped at the next door down the hall. "Okay, I'm opening the door now," she said looking directly at me and Mrs. Presley. She kept staring but didn't move.

"Um, great," I said. "Open away."

Smiling still, she opened the door slowly and poked her head inside. Then, seemingly satisfied with whatever she saw or didn't see inside, she opened it all the way. She reached to a panel just inside the door, and the room was suddenly bathed in warm light. "This room doesn't get much use."

I looked around in dismay. The "disused" room was equipped with two double beds. You didn't often see that outside of a hotel room. But that's where the similarity to a hotel ended. Or at least any hotels I was familiar with.

The beds were elegant but looked sturdy enough. The night table between them was exquisite. Probably not Dix-proof. The vanity and matching chair at the end of the room were definitely not Dix-proof. They looked incredibly delicate. And valuable. As did the lamps and the artwork on the wall. Oh, the havoc I could wreak there...

Mrs. Presley walked over to the nearest bed, hiked her butt up on it, and did the sit-bounce comfort test on the mattress. "Dibs on this one."

"We're sharing a room?" I asked.

Caryn nodded. "Hope that's all right."

"Perfectly all right," Mrs. P said. "I like to keep this one close...keep an eye on her. Her being such a wild one and all."

Okay, I had asked her to roll with the role...but come on!

"The bathroom is right through there." Caryn directed our attention to one of the doors off to the side. "Feel free to use the dressers and the closet, of course. If you need anything laundered, just let me know in the morning. I'll see to it."

Caryn turned back around with the satisfied smile of someone who really knew her job and enjoyed it.

"You've thought of everything," Mrs P said.

Caryn smiled. "I try to. And I'm just two doors down the hall on your right if you need anything in the night."

That surprised me. Not that Caryn would volunteer to assist us with any problems we might have, but that she was on this floor with the family. Before I could frame a discreet question on the matter—because let's face it, I'm not exactly the queen of discreet—Caryn supplied the answer.

"I used to have a room downstairs, in the housekeepers' quarters. But I'm the only full-time, live-in staff, and Hugh likes us all close. So I moved up a short while ago."

"Was that when you hurt your back?"

Caryn didn't blink as she looked at me. But her lips thinned, and her confident smile dimmed.

"Yes," she said. "When I hurt my back."

"Slipped a disc or something?" I fished for more information.

She nodded. "Something like that."

She wasn't volunteering any information, and I would be indiscreet to ask how she'd done it.

"How did you do it?"

Long live the queen of indiscreet.

Caryn drew a tight breath as she walked toward the door. "Accidents happen."

"What was the accident?"

"Nothing really."

"But how—"

Slam. She was out the door.

"Geez, why the big mystery over how she hurt her back?" I plunked down on the empty bed across from Mrs. P and stared up at the ceiling.

"Get off your butt and give me a hand, Dix."

I turned to see what she was talking about. "Help you with what?"

Mrs. Presley was moving furniture. Specifically, that very spindly looking nightstand between the beds.

"Hell," she said. "Rich people don't know how to decorate. This room is atrocious. Come help me."

That nightstand wasn't the only thing we moved. It was just the first. There was a delicate tall lamp in the corner. I guessed the Drammens hadn't just run down to Costco to pick that baby up. Following Mrs. P's direction, I put it in the closet. There was a fancy swag lamp over my bed. It was hung there by a solid-looking iron rod. Yeah, did not want that coming down on my head.

"Well, that's got to go," Mrs. Presley said. Apparently she wasn't in favor of me cracking my head either.

She probably didn't want to be woken up by the noise.

A pair of framed prints was the next to go into the closet. Next, the ever-vigilant Mrs. Presley suggested we roll up the small Persian rugs on the floor. She didn't want either of us taking a midnight slip and slide.

"But if I did go ass over kettle, you'd break my fall like Elizabeth did Hugh's, right Dix?"

"Sure, Mrs. P," I said, slowly and with as much sarcasm as I could muster. "Sure I would."

Well, truthfully, I would.

I bent, pulled up the first mat, and laughed.

Mrs. P was folding her ironed undies into the top dresser drawer. "What's so funny?"

"Look," I said. "Toilet seat covers for your troll dolls?"

"What are you talking about?"

I flipped the mat over to show her. Round rubber rings had been glued to the back of the mat—one at each corner, and a couple more in the center.

"Huh. Rubber washers." Mrs. Presley grabbed one up, examining the handiwork. "Wonder why Caryn used these?"

"Well, I'm guessing so the mats wouldn't slide around."

"Of course. And it's a pretty good idea, actually. Economical too. I just would have expected some kind of non-slip underlay or something."

We finished rolling up the rugs, and I stashed them under my bed.

Now that Mrs. Presley was seemingly done giving me orders, I looked around the large bedroom. Perfect. If my REM sleep disorder kicked in and I started thrashing around, the most valuable stuff had been stashed or moved out of range. Nothing would be falling on me. There wasn't anything that I could possibly destroy if I flailed around in bed. And if I were to swing at the wall in my sleep, well, it would have to be with one hell of a reach to connect. We'd moved the bed away from the wall.

Mrs. Presley had jumped in and done it for me without

having to be asked.

"Thanks, Mrs. P."

She looked at me as if I were crazy.

"For what?" she asked. "For taking up your end of the lifting?"

"Right. That's exactly what I meant." There was no way in a million years she'd admit to actually helping me out. Yet again.

The sudden blare of Elvis singing "Jailhouse Rock" jangled in the momentary silence. The King himself? No, Mrs. P's cell phone.

"That'll be one of the boys," she said. "I was supposed to call as soon as I got here. They'll both be all shook up. Get it, Dix? All shook up?"

Why yes, it does go beyond her wearing of blue suede shoes. She rummaged through her purse, extracted her phone, and told Cal to wait while she waved me out the door.

"Get going. You've reading to catch up on, don't you?"

Indeed I did.

As Mrs. P consoled a lonesome Cal, I slipped out into the hallway. All doors were firmly shut, and only dim lighting from three pot lights overhead illuminated the way. The elevator? Though I had no less than ten "going down" lines I was dying to try out on Dylan, I decided on the stairs. As quiet as the elevator was, it did make a slight gear-whirring noise and probably generated vibration in the floors. I did not want anyone alerted that I was up and about, sneaking around Drammen House like some cat burglar.

Yeah, that's it. Like some drop-dead gorgeous, stealthily inclined, sexy, Spandex-wearing burglar who'd stop at nothing to get what she wanted.

Okay, so I wasn't wearing Spandex—that was for twenty-year-old butts—but the rest of it was apt. Ish.

When I reached the first floor, I made a beeline to Hugh's study. With any luck...yes! The door wasn't just unlocked, it was ajar. I did a mental fist pump. Hugh Drammen was a very trusting soul.

I peered around the dim study.

Ah, there was the reason for the unlocked door. Humphrey. I could make out the outline of the dog comfortably ensconced on a plush dog bed by the patio doors. I could also hear him gently snoring. Draped in cozy moonlight, he was doubtlessly still sleeping off the soporific effects of the stout he'd lapped up. Everything in the room was where it should be again. Almost everything. The mat that had slipped out from under Hugh's feet was draped over a small drying rack.

I probably could have turned on a low lamp. The whole household seemed to have called it a night, so there wasn't much risk of being discovered. No, the real reason I wanted to leave the light off was that Dylan was still in training. Yes, yes, we were partners. But I was the senior partner. Senior as in more experienced! Not as in get your card out at the local diner for ten percent off any meal before four o'clock.

I wanted to surprise Dylan in the dark. Sneak up on him when he entered the room. Yes, that's right—teach him to be on the lookout for surprises. On guard at all times.

You guessed it...that whole competitive thing I've got going on.

However, Dylan Foreman can be just as competitive.

I had planned to hide under the desk in that hee-hee-hee-I'm-so-clever way I have of doing ...well, okay, of doing everything. Hugh's desk was huge, one of those wrap around ones under which you just know every executive with a lockable office door keeps a sleeping bag.

Oh, and Doritos.

I got down on my hands and knees and started to crawl in but stopped. It was not quite as spacious as I imagined it would be, so I decided to back in rather than get in there and try to turn around. It just about killed me not to make those *beep beep, beep* backing up noises.

And maybe I should have. Because I bumped into something—or rather someone—almost immediately. My heart jumped. Then a pair of hands landed on my butt. A pair of unmistakeable hands that began doing wonderful things to me. I froze in place as a pair of arms came around me, finding other sensitive places. Any minute now, I'd feel the brush of that fake moustache on my neck...

"Oh, Allen, we'll have to be quiet. My boyfriend might hear us."

"Oh, your boyfriend, huh?" Dylan said. "What's he got that I haven't got?"

"Chaps."

"Huh?"

"Chaps. I love 'em."

"Only chaps? That's it?"

"Well, he is very tall and handsome, virile…"

On *virile*, I felt his hands tighten on my waist. I grabbed one of those hands and planted it on my left breast. "Tell me, Allen, what do you think of this substandard breast? Would you call it unremarkable?"

Dylan snorted. "You're not going to let that go, are you?"

"Let it go?" I scoffed. "It's like you don't even know me."

"Say," he said. "I never did give you that Valentine's Day gift."

"That's right," I said. "You didn't. You owe me. Big time."

Oh, how I hoped it was time for Big Time! And yes, that is a pet name for a certain part of his anatomy.

Honestly it had been awhile since we'd had sex. I mean since we'd had down-and-dirty, grind-one-out sex. I so wanted to jump him.

"What did the hot-blooded PI in the elevator say to his ultra-sexy girlfriend on their three month anniversary, which happens to coincide with Valentine's Day?"

I gulped. "Out of service?" He was doing remarkable things to that breast with his hand.

"Nope, not even close." He pulled back so I could turn around and stretch out on the carpet.

"Next stop, plumbing and heating?"

"Sorry." On hands and knees, he moved up my body to nuzzle my neck.

"Penthouse?" I guessed, my voice high and thin.

"Penthouse?" He lifted his head. "No, Dix. That lucky guy said *time to go down*."

Damn, he'd beat me to the elevator punch line. Except as he started to slide back down my body, I somehow didn't care about losing that one.

CHAPTER 6

I'D CALLED MY mother when Dylan and I had gotten together. She'd sent chocolate-covered cherries. Oh man, they were so yummy I'd wondered if I should break up with Dylan for half a day or something just so we could get back together and she'd send us some more.

Yes, us.

I had shared them with Dylan. Well, we were a "couple." It seemed like the right thing to do.

Also, he'd been right there at the office when UPS made the delivery and had seen me open the parcel. He spotted the chocolates before I could snap the lid closed. So I pretty much had to share.

Come on, did you think I'd share chocolate-covered cherries willingly?

Anyway, we'd had the sweet little treat with a nice red wine. Yes, I always keep a bottle in my desk. We were relaxing in my office, which afforded a modicum of privacy. It was late in the afternoon, but people were still milling about the old building. The main door to Dodd and Foreman was unlocked...and we decided to play the chocolate covered cherry game.

It was Dylan's suggestion.

Oh hell, it was Dylan's game—made up on the spot.

I was up for it, naturally. Though to be honest, when he'd first suggested we play a game with the gift, I thought he meant sucking off the chocolate and spitting the cherries at each other in some weird adaptation of dodge ball.

Did I mention we'd gotten into the wine?

But he had another idea—an infinitely better one. Kind of like playing chicken. You know, strategically placing a chocolate cherry on a part of one's anatomy—don't think eye sockets, that's just sick!—and daring the other to nibble it off. Or suck it off for extra points. I must admit it got fun.

Then it got kind of dangerous. No, not choke-on-a-cherry dangerous (and wow, that would be a mood killer, wouldn't it?). Nor were either of us in danger of falling down a well. But what if that office door flew open and someone caught us? At any moment, someone could have come charging through that unlocked door and forged on into my office when they found the outer office unmanned.

Yes, Blow-Up Betty was on guard duty, but she's not the most attentive of blow-up dolls. Anyone at all could have come through that door and seen us in various states of undress, sipping our wine, playing our games...nibbling away at the...nibbly bits.

That just made it all the hotter.

I enjoy that little bit of daring. That little bit of worry that we might get caught. That little bit of hurry. But now, under Hugh Drammen's desk, while we were on a case, while anyone in the household could come in and catch us, well, that was even steamier.

How daring did we dare get?

As it happened, pretty daring.

"You didn't get me, Dix," Dylan said.

I blinked. I distinctly recalled him getting off. Unless he meant...

"What? Is there some kind of oral sex bank that I don't know about?" I said. "You do me, and automatically, I—"

"God, no. That's not what I meant." Dylan ran a hand through his stupendously messed hair. Damn, the guy would have reverse male pattern baldness if he dated me much longer. "First of all, if there was some sort of oral sex bank, you'd know about it."

Know about it? I'd be a freakin' shareholder.

"Secondly, what I meant was, you didn't trip me up in the dark. You were crawling under this desk to try to surprise me, to catch me unaware when I came in the room. But, I turned the tables on you. *I* caught *you* off guard."

"Ha! In your face, Dylan Foreman!" Um. Okay, considering what we'd just been doing, that may not have been the most eloquent statement I'd ever made. On the other hand, I'm not known for eloquent statements. "I repeat: In. Your. Face! I knew you were under this desk all along."

"Really?"

"Really."

Not really.

Okay, so he was right. He'd gotten the upper hand on me that time. The apprentice had outshone the master. Though I wouldn't admit to it under threat of torture by *Saved by the Bell* reruns. But was I upset by that?

Pfffft! Did you miss that part about what happened under the desk?

And besides, I had other things on my mind...like how would one go about opening up a bank for—

"This is so great, huh?"

Dylan's words pulled my enterprising mind back to reality.

"What's so great?"

"Us. We're so great."

I looked at him. Us? Yeah, we were still sort of tangled under Hugh's desk. Limbs entangled, jeans torn asunder, underwear...balled up in the leg of them. Moustache…? On his right cheek.

With a rip and a re-press, I fixed it for him. Then we both crawled out from under the desk and started to shimmy back into our clothes.

Dylan's words sank in. *Us. We're so great.*

Crap, I knew what he was going to say next. One of two things: either he wanted to talk about that cursed camping trip with his law buddies or else he wanted to take that elevator down again. I stilled with my hands on the button of my jeans.

"Um, can it wait?"

"Again, with the wait!" He threw his hands in the air. "I want to talk about that camping trip, Dix."

Well there you go. Asked and answered. I did up the button on my jeans. Or rather I tried to do it up. Dammit! Why had I chosen to wear such a tight pair? Oh right, Dix hadn't chosen them. D had. Getting into those babies had been a major contortionist's job. I'd done a half dozen jump-suck-pull/jump-suck-pulls before I'd hauled up that zipper earlier. They were a little looser now, but it was still going to take some work.

Great. Just what I wanted Dylan to see.

Not!

"Quick, look over there." I pointed to the patio doors.

He didn't turn. "What? Distraction? You think that'll end the argument."

If it worked…

"What I think is we're supposed to be investigating things here. We don't know how much time that's going to take." Hey, I had a point. I mean...we were basically breaking into the old guy's office. And we'd just done some pretty fun stuff under his desk. "We really should get investigating."

Dylan knew I was right. But he didn't like it. "Why don't you even want to talk about it?"

"Talk about what? Hockey? Sorry, not into it. The forecast? Dark. Oh, maybe we could have a rousing discussion on math? Like in Y - ½ + 9 = legit. Oh and just so you know...I'm the Y! That's right," I said dramatically. "Why me? Y...me!"

That shut him up for a moment.

Shut me up too. Me and my big mouth. And lack of math skills.

"I'll go check out the patio doors." Dylan turned away.

I jump-pulled my jeans and managed to button the button on the first try, but I felt in no way victorious.

Yes, I *had* wanted to divert Dylan's attention while I got back into my skinny jeans with as little embarrassment as possible, but that wasn't the only reason. Personal feelings aside, we really had to get our examination of the room started.

There'd been a fire here two nights before. Elizabeth swore Hugh hadn't set it, accidentally or otherwise, and every bone in my body—which was one less now than it had been fifteen minutes before—was telling me she was right. Caryn had raced in that patio door after the fire had started. Was that how the arsonist had gotten in?

"Anything?" I asked.

There might have been tension between us a few minutes before, but now we were back to professionalism. Pure professionalism.

I grabbed a rubber band from the desk and snapped it in his direction. It caught him in the thigh.

He slanted me a reproving look and turned back to the door.

Okay, now we were back to pure professionalism.

He'd opened the French doors and was examining the lock, latch, and casing, using a penlight he'd taken from his pocket to get a closer look.

Elizabeth had told us—and thankfully she was right!—that the doors and windows of the mansion were not alarmed. Apparently Hugh-Bear had steadfastly refused to have any kind of security installed. If the wrought iron fence surrounding the estate and the security guard stationed behind a bank of security monitors in the gatehouse weren't enough to stop an intruder, an alarm system would present no obstacle. An alarm system would, however, impede Hugh and Humphrey's comings and goings.

Dylan closed the door quietly and pocketed his penlight. "Nothing here, Dix. No evidence of tampering or anything else."

I nodded and walked over to him. Humphrey looked up at us, decided we weren't worth the effort of getting up, and laid his head back down.

I pulled out my penlight and shone it through the glass panes of the French door to the walkway outside. I was hoping to see footprints in the snow. There had been no fresh snowfall since the fire, and I knew that Caryn had purportedly rushed in that door. But there were no tracks to be seen. Just a well-shoveled stone path leading away from the house. My flashlight's beam wasn't powerful enough to show where it led, but I knew there were a ton of walkways out there. I'd noticed it when we'd come in earlier.

"Morris does a good job," Dylan said.

He was right. The corners of the walkway were shovelled square, the path was wide. There wasn't a bit of dog poo in sight. Just the cobblestone path through the snow, fading into darkness.

We turned our attention back to the room.

I reached for the mat draped on the drying rack I'd noticed earlier. No surprise, it was still damp. I held it to my face and inhaled. Chlorine. Caryn had washed it.

"Hey what are these rubber things on the back?" Dylan asked.

"Toilet seats for little troll dolls."

Seriously creepy, creepy dolls.

Dylan grinned, and I grinned back at him.

Yes, part of it was the high of an investigation in progress. There's always a thrill to sleuthing about in the dead of night.

But I knew too that part of it was his way of calling a truce after our tiff. I handed the mat over to him.

He examined it and rubbed the fingers of his right hand together. "There's some sort of sticky stuff on my fingers."

"Well, Dylan, when a man and a women get together in that special way, there are certain body fluids that—"

He rolled his eyes. "From the mat, Dix."

Oh, adhesive. Right.

He hung the mat back on the rack, just as neatly lined up as we'd found it.

Now for the nitty-gritty of the investigation—we went over to where the fire had burned.

Without a word between us, Dylan grabbed an end of the couch and I took the other. On a silent count of three, we lifted/slid it out from the wall and then moved in behind it.

Dylan pulled out his penlight again and shone it on the charred shelf.

Two shelves above the burned shelf—nothing. No damage whatsoever. The fire had definitely started on just that one shelf. Even the board immediately above hadn't been too badly burned, so it had to have been contained quickly. I glanced around at the expensive-looking books that lined two full walls of the room. It could have been so much worse.

"So we know where it started," I said.

"But how?"

Elizabeth had rejected the idea of a candle as the cause of the fire. She had to be right—the fire started on the flat bottom of the shelf, not higher up.

Smoking? I'd seen chain smokers leave lit cigarettes on counters. But according to Elizabeth, no one in the house smoked.

Cooking? Maybe old Hugh was grilling himself a panini to go with Humphrey's pickles and crackers and forgot about it? That didn't seem likely either. He just did not look like a panini kind of guy.

That left—

"Arson," Dylan said. "This fire had to have been deliberately set."

"Elizabeth said Hugh was alone in here when the fire broke out..."

"And yet he slept through someone walking in, leaning over the couch where he slept, and setting some books on fire?" Dylan shook his head. "I'm not buying it."

I smiled. "Right. But you don't believe any more than I do that he started that fire himself. Especially not with his dog in here with him."

Dylan paced—that always helped him to think. And I watched him pace—that worked for me. Then he came to a sudden stop and laughed.

"What?"

"Maybe there really is a fire-starting/telekinesis kid around here, like Mrs. P said when we were driving in. Doing this stuff with their mind."

"Yes!" I feigned my exuberance. "And it worked on time delay too? Someone came in here, bored their beady, blazing gaze into that spot just above Hugh's head, and...waited."

Ah, there was that feeling.

I'd been joking around. But the more I thought about it...not so much.

Dylan picked up on it right away. "Are you thinking someone set the fire by some delayed method?"

"Basically...yeah."

"Look here," Dylan had been moving the penlight slowly; he stopped all together.

I saw it immediately. There was a small, unburned square on the wood, about half the size of a postage stamp.

"What was here?" he asked.

I shook my head. I didn't know. But I knew it was something ....

In the hallway, the grandfather clocked started its midnight chiming. But as it progressed, it sounded weirdly. I listened a little closer, and—yes, I trust my intuition—it sounded warningly.

And I swear it was then, not before, trailing behind that penetrating blip of intuition, that I heard the footsteps in the hallway beyond the door.

"Dylan, listen."

He stood perfectly still, and it didn't take a shitload of intuition to know when he felt/heard the footsteps too. He made a beeline for under the desk, and I was right behind him. Did I mention I was wearing too-tight jeans? Yeah, they unsnapped as I dove. The zipper slid down with an audible rasp.

"Geez, Dix," Dylan whispered. "Now?"

"Of course not now! Unless you were thinking—"

"Shhhh!"

The door opened. I waited a few seconds for a light to come on, but the room remained in darkness. Whoever had joined us in Hugh's study wasn't supposed to be in there either. So would they run for the patio door? Hugh's mini bar? Or maybe grab a book off the shelf, or—

Crap! I heard the footsteps tiptoeing softly across the carpet toward the desk. I caught the faint whiff of a rosy perfume. Female intruder, definitely.

But who?

I pressed myself back against the desk's modesty panel as Hugh's chair pulled out. We held perfectly still as someone sat down. Sock-clad feet toed the carpet. A desk drawer slid open…

"Now where would he put it?" she whispered.

Dylan and I exchanged a quick glance. We'd not heard that particular voice before.

Then a light clicked on—a tall lamp behind Hugh's chair. We held our breath, but the intruder didn't see us. Probably too focused on whatever she was searching for in Hugh's desk.

Clunk.

I started as a backpack dropped to the floor in front of us.

The front pouch was open, and the contents spilled. Thanks to the light from the lamp, I could identify some of the jumble. A bunch of coins, a large clunky bracelet, two bottles of nail polish, tiny nail scissors, a glitzy nail file, one three-inch chandelier earring, half a crumpled joint.

Then a delicate hand came down to gather up the spilled contents, and I got a good look at those nails. Those gorgeous inch-long fingernails. But then those gathering hands stopped. Whoever was at Hugh's desk went perfectly quiet. Oh damn, I knew that stilled posture!

We'd been nabbed.

Roma Drammen's hand shot back down, and she dug her long, shiny, slick nails-of-freakin'-steel into the back of my hand.

CHAPTER 7

BUSTED. DAMMIT!

Me. Of all people!

Hey, Dix Dodd doesn't do caught on the job! Except when she does...but that's in those rare, rare instances. Like the time that gorgeous Hollywood actor was doing a shoot in Toronto and wanted me to find out what his model girlfriend was doing while he flexed.

As it turned out, the producer's son.

Yes, I got caught. On scene. The smash through-the-window, set-fire-to-the-tour-bus scene that they had to reshoot.

Or like the time when I was working at Jones and Associates. I'd been sent out on a rinky-dink assignment to follow an extreme right-wing politician into a local establishment of questionable repute. Problem was, Stoner Stan and I go way back. He waved me over right away. Asked me how my day had gone. Did I catch that *Big Bang* rerun? Had I heard from Peaches Marie lately? And—argggggh!—how was work in the gumshoe business?

And dammit, like now, as Roma Drammen dug, dug, dug her death grip into my hand.

"Okay, okay," I said. "I'm coming out."

Roma loosened her grip. She dropped her head down—thankfully, still attached to her neck—and looked at us. Her long auburn curls nearly touched the floor.

"Don't you mean '*we're* coming out'? I see two bodies under there."

"Fine."

"And with your hands up!" Roma said. She stood and stepped back from the desk.

Hands up? Wasn't that a little overdramatic?

"Well un-nail my hand, and we will."

Once I was free, Dylan and I crawled out from under the desk. Yikes, my hand hurt like hell. But that was the least of my worries.

Time to get ready for the twenty questions...followed by the twenty quickest lies that I hoped wouldn't sink us.

"Aren't you two a little old for this?"

She glanced down at my unsnapped, zipper-sliding jeans.

"Oh for God sake," she said. "Lower your hands and zip up your pants."

Brilliant. Roma Drammen thought she'd caught us having sex under her grandfather's desk. Little did she know…

Dylan and I stood there and waited for the shit-storm to begin. Well, sort of waited for it. But not so much, especially as the seconds ticked on. Roma was looking like a woman who'd been caught doing something she shouldn't too.

She looked at me. "Geez, lady, I said zip up your pants."

"She means you, D," Dylan said.

Was he trying to be funny?

Okay, it was a little funny.

"I know who you are," Roma said. But she didn't say it in that suddenly dawning way. It was a statement. "You're D Bee. Mom emailed me that you were here. Um, aren't you going to zip up?"

I'd been trying! Seriously, all that time.

Time for drastic measures. I squatted down, stood back up pulling, pulling, pulling. And miracle of miracles—yes, I'd done a squat. Oh, and I'd loosened my jeans just enough so that maybe if I sucked my belly in as hard as I could, and yanked real hard—

Dammit.

"No," I said. "I'm not going to button them up." I pulled my shirt down to cover the unbuttoned waistband.

"Mom told me you were—"

"A loose woman? A wild one? A cougar?"

"Elizabeth's mother," she finished "I saw you at the wedding."

Okay, I was really tanking.

So I sat. Well, it was more of an exasperated fall into the leather of Hugh's couch than graciously taking a seat, but it was apparently all the signal Roma had needed that the conversation had gone casual.

Since I'd made no introduction, Dylan took care of that himself. "I'm Magnus. Magnus Quinn."

"Roma Drammen."

She perched on the edge of her grandfather's desk, crossed her spindly legs, and wrapped her hands around her knee. Then she began bobbing her foot. "Was that your PB?"

Dylan and I exchanged confused glances.

I tried to guess. "Peanut butter and …."

Roma rolled her eyes. "No. Your personal best."

"Our personal best what?" Dylan asked.

"You know...sex?"

Were we supposed to answer that? I mean it was great, but there was that time after a Stones concert—

After...during...yeah, somewhere in between there.

"Don't answer that, D," Dylan said.

Does the guy know me or what?

"My boyfriend Dax and I play all the time," Roma said,

clearly more interested in sharing her details than waiting for ours. “Dax says our personal best was that time when we did it on his mother’s wool coat in the coat closet at his great uncle’s funeral.” She pulled a sudden, solemn face and put a hand to her heart. “God rest his soul.”

Oh, that made it better.

“But hey,” Roma continued. “If anyone tells you grey wool’s good for the knees, they’re lying.”

I would remember that.

“Magnus, forget she said that,” I whispered.

Roma continued, “ But that’s just Dax’s opinion. To my way of thinking, nothing trumped that time in the science library, back in September. And why the hell put tables in the conference rooms if they don’t want us to use them?”

She had a point.

“Hey, did you know library people don’t get true love?” she said.

“I heard that,” I said, congenially. “Totally agree.”

“It’s like a rule or something they learn at library school. Same with Campus Security. Seriously, no hearts. The jerks.”

This was working out better than I’d thought. Perhaps the chatty young lady could provide a wealth of information. And it told me something else. Her mother had also given her the low-down on my sexual awesomeness...though Tammy may not have used those exact words.

“I’m with you on that.” Dylan must have been thinking the same thing I was. “Campus security can be such—”

“Dicks!” Roma cut in.

“What?” I said.

Her eyes narrowed as she looked at me. “What do you mean—what?”

Crap! She’d said *dicks*, not *Dix*. Plural rather than me—one of a kind.

“I mean...what is up with those security dicks, right?”

Oh, those eyes were narrowing. Suspicion was pouring in.

“Under the desk?” Dylan asked, clearly as a distraction.

"You thought that was our personal best? Pfft! Not even close."

"Oooh." Roma adjusted herself on the desk, sitting up a little straighter. Or grinding into the wood. I get those two confused. "Details."

"Under this desk was not even close to our personal best," Dylan said. "D and I were out camping with a bunch of old friends. And while they were out skating, we did it…" He glanced at me in the dramatic pause. "...back at the chalet, up in a loft overlooking the lake."

"Is that it?" Roma did not look impressed.

"Well, yeah," Dylan said.

"Did you leave your socks on or something?" she asked. "Now that would be hot. Not adventurist, but hot. I love guys in socks."

My heart skipped a solid beat. Did I have a long lost little sister?

Dylan's arm was quick around me. God, he must have known I was feeling a little light-headed there.

"Anyway." Roma jumped off the desk and grabbed her bag. "I've gotta scram. Dax should be outside by now. But first, a word of advice."

I shrugged. "Sure."

"You'd better clear out of this room before my mom catches you in here."

I paused. "But I thought she'd gone to bed for the night?"

"She roams this place all night long." Roma tossed the words over her shoulder as she walked toward the door. "It's like...like she's some kind of demented...ghost or something. Very weird."

"Did she always do that?" I asked.

Roma paused. "No, just since November, I think."

November. Seems it had been a banner month in Drammen-land.

Roma flipped a wave our way. "See ya!"

"Wait," Dylan said. "What were you doing here?"

Damned good question. Dylan had said it with imposed authority. Yes, so often that worked. But not with Roma.

"Dudes, I *live* here. It's my house."

"You were going through your grandfather's desk drawers," I said.

She shrugged. "He's my grandfather."

"Sneaking into his study?" I said. "Unless you've got Dax somewhere behind you, I'm guessing you weren't playing the PB game."

"Why I was going through the desk is my business." Her eyes grew suddenly wide. "You can't tell my parents I'm here."

Ah, the good old upper hand. I hesitated, thinking this through. "Here, as in the study? Or as in the house?"

"Both." She let out an exasperated sigh. "I've been here a few weeks. Caryn's the only one who knows."

"How could you be living here and your parents not know?"

"I come and go. Sleep all day, sneak out to party at night. Big house. Busy people. Four bathrooms," she answered.

"And you haven't told your folks yet?" I guessed. "That you're not in school anymore."

"They'll freak. Guaranteed total fa-reak."

Well, we couldn't have that. And I wanted to keep this ally.

"Okay," I said. "I won't tell your parents."

"Oh, you misunderstand," Roma said. "When I said you can't tell my parents, I wasn't *asking* you not to tell. I'm *telling* you not to tell. Tell them I'm here, and I'll tell them you were banging your boy toy partner under my grandfather's desk. And that you're not related to Elizabeth. At all. Neither is that older lady you brought around."

I was stunned. "How did you—"

"I know things the same way you do," she said to me. Roma looked around the room. "If you pulled any books out, better make sure to put them back exactly as you found them. You know how it is with obsessive folk. They go a little nutty over the slightest difference."

"Just one question," I said. "Where were you when the fire started in here?"

"Up in the room you're sleeping in tonight. The guest room. Mom goes into my room all the time, but the guest room—nope."

Another thought struck me. "Roma, where are the books that caught fire? Did your mom mention that in her email?"

"Elizabeth took them."

"Where?"

She reached and snapped off the lamp behind her grandfather's chair, plunging the room into darkness again. Then she opened the door and light from the hallway spilled in. Not much light but enough so that I could clearly see the smirk on her face. "She goes jogging every morning at five forty. Why don't you follow her and find out?"

She closed the door behind her.

Dylan looked at me. "How did she know that? About us?"

I knew the answer. Not only was she a sock-loving soul sister, that young lady was like me in another way. She was extremely intuitive.

It was kind of cool. Intriguing. Fun.

And annoying as hell.

CHAPTER 8

WHEN I WENT to bed that night, I set my clock. My internal clock, that is. It's just another cool mental ability we ace PIs have. Comes from strange shifts and the lulls in stakeouts. So, yes, I set that alarm in my mind for five twenty, and when five twenty came...I kept on sleeping.

Luckily, I'd set my cell phone too. It went off at five twenty-two.

Okay, so I didn't have that internal alarm down pat just yet.

To be fair to me, I had spent a great deal of time that night listening for movement outside my bedroom door in the hallway. Had Roma been exaggerating about her mother's nocturnal shuffling around? My instinct told me she hadn't been. And my instinct was second to none. None!

Right?

I wasn't about to get into an intuition pissing contest with Roma Drammen. But wow, it's kind of rare to meet another person with that particular gift. It was blowing my mind a little bit. Just how well could she instinctively read others? Most importantly, how well could she read me?

Anyway, back to my internal clock. As I said, it didn't alert me at five twenty. So instead of me being able to tiptoe out of the room, letting Mrs. P sleep, both of us were jolted awake by my cell phone ring tone, which was currently set to Skyler's voice from *Breaking Bad* screaming Shut-up! Shut-up! Shut-up!

"What the holy hell is that?" Mrs. P said.

"Just my phone alarm. Go back to sleep Mrs. P."

"No. Once I'm up, I'm up." She stretched. "But I slept like a baby, that's for sure."

I offered a sheepish half apology for the early wake up, accompanied by a very generous offer to let her have the bathroom first.

"No, I'm good," she said. She snuggled down deeper under the blankets. "Already went. Wonder where we could get new sheets?"

There was a frightened pause—and that was mine. "So when you say you *already went…*"

"About an hour ago."

"Okay, but when you wonder where we could get new sheets…"

"Not for me, Dix. For you. You were tossing and turning all night. The way you were going at it, I thought you might have torn the fitted one.

I shot up. Crap. "Did I break anything?"

Mrs. P sat up too and turned on her bedside light. I took a look around. Nothing broken, nothing knocked over. Something different? By the balcony doors there had been a small sofa. The lavender cushions and paisley throw pillows were on the floor beside my bed. They hadn't been there when I'd gone to sleep. Mrs. Presley must have set them out after I'd finally turned in, just in case.

She was one good lady. Kind when you weren't looking. Sweet when no one could tell.

Had I ever told her these things? Should I? Hell, no! She'd kill me.

I looked down at my purse as I swung out of bed.

Ah, and there was the FUD. I picked it up.

Maybe Dylan had meant to order FUDGE. Yeah, that was it. He'd wanted to buy fudge off the internet.

My gaze went back to the FUD. I bit down on my lip. Should I try it out? I mean, it wasn't the worst idea in the world. It might come in handy one day.

I grabbed it from my purse and, pressing it out of sight against my leg, headed to the bathroom.

The one thing that my little condo lacks is a nice en suite bathroom. The one in that Drammen guest room was small, equipped only with a shower, not a full bath, but it was finished very nicely. Very expensively. The countertop was an ivory-colored marble, the fixtures burnished nickel. The sink was one of those affairs that sat on top of the countertop like a beautiful white porcelain bowl. Big, plush, white towels were stacked on a shelf beneath the sink. The walls were a lovely pale yellow. Several mirrors, framed in black, made the room look larger than it actually was. Even the toilet looked elegant.

I shut the bathroom door behind me—a couple times, thanks to the stupid latch that didn't catch quite right—and walked across the cold tile floor to the toilet.

I'm not really one to notice those things normally, but the room was poorly laid out. As I stood there facing the toilet, I came face to face with myself in that early morning hour. No, it wasn't one of those Zen reality things. Not even an Oprah aha moment. I was literally seeing my reflection. What genius thought it was a good idea to hang a mirror up over the toilet? Did guys check out their receding hairlines as they peed?

I shook my head. Sometimes I just didn't get men. And on that cheery note, I looked again at the FUD. I drew down the front of my grey sweats and placed the so-not-fudge contraption...um...strategically. Then I waited.

And waited a few seconds more. I had to admit, it was awkward. Seriously, my natural instincts were telling me to clench right up.

What could I do to coax it along?

Should I whistle? Isn't there some sort of urban myth about whistling?

But as I waited, I checked myself out in the mirror again. This time, I gazed deep into my eyes. Well, after admiring my hairline. It is pretty nice, if I do say so myself.

Dylan.

Yes, I was thinking of him. More specifically, I was thinking how much I really wanted to move that bathroom mirror over the toilet at his place now. And yes, I was also thinking about how he wanted us to take things further. He wanted me to—dear God—take a leap of faith.

And then something happened.

In that mirror, I saw something I'd never seen before. And kind of never-fucking-ever wanted to see again! No, not just the stream of urine now flowing like a mighty waterfall. When I glanced up in the mirror again, it was to see the door slowly creaking open. Damn that latch! And there stood a shocked Mrs. Presley watching me tinkle into the toilet.

I couldn't just stop mid-stream! God, maybe men *weren't* lying when they said their dick had a mind of its own.

Damn!

Mrs. Presley paled. Her eyes grew wider than I'd ever seen them. "Dix! You're...you're…"

She looked up; she looked down. Up at my face, then down to my—

"This isn't what you think!" I hurried to say. "I got it from Dylan!"

"Lord, Dix! What are you doing? Collecting them?"

It was right about then that I started to blabber a little less coherently. It all came spilling out. About our little anniversaries that still scared me just enough every time the fourteenth rolled around. About card shops and Stoner Stan's and thimbles and cookies and yes, female urination devices.

Oh. And winter camping trips.

I drew a deep breath as I finally ran down...or out.

"Do you want to run that by me again?" Mrs. P asked. She was smiling.

No. I positively did not want to run that by her again.

I finished with the FUD and repositioned my sweatpants, but not before contemplating that age-old question: do I shake it or not? Shrugging, I washed both the FUD and my hands. And yes, I did shake the water droplets off it. If the thing was going back in my purse, it was going in clean and dry.

I made my awkward way back to the bedroom. Mrs. P, having abandoned her inadvertent post outside the bathroom door, was sitting on her bed now, wiping the tears of mirth from her eyes.

"For a moment, I thought you were growing parts." She sat on the bed, clutching a pillow as she laughed. "I know some pretty strange things can happen to us when we reach a certain age, but growing a...growing a—"

She dissolved into giggles again before she could say *penis*, but I stood frozen with horror. *What* strange things could happen? *Like growing a nut sack?*

I'd been having a dream lately about that happening to me. The nut sack thing, I mean. So often, in fact, that it had become a positive phobia. Was it even physically *possible* to grow a nut sack? I mean, *spontaneously*?

A few minutes later, Mrs. P's laughter had subsided. But that broad grin remained.

"Dix, relax," Mrs. P said. "I knew what was going on the moment that old door creaked itself open and I accidentally got a peek. I've seen stranger devices than that in all my years in the no-tell motel business."

Oh, I bet she had.

"So," she said. "Tell me about this camping trip."

Argh! Me and my big mouth.

"You're going, right?" Mrs. P asked. "This sounds like something Dylan really wants."

"I don't know."

"Well, you know what I think. I think that you—"

"I know what you're going to say, Mrs. P. That I shouldn't be so scared to make this leap of faith."

"No, I was going to say you shouldn't be so scared to take a stand...get it? Take a stand, as in standing up to—"

"Yeah, I got it, Mrs. Presley." I just couldn't bring myself to call her Mrs. *P* right then. "But it's not that easy."

Mrs. Presley smiled. "It never is."

"Yes, but I've been burned so—"

"So you get to be the exception to the rule?"

"The rule?" I asked. "Which rule is that?"

"The one that says when you get burned, you cry your eyes out with someone who cares about you. Sit down, drink the beverage of your choice, and cry some more. But then you get over it. You blow your nose on his best shirt and leave it hanging in the closet."

"Oh, that rule."

Mrs. Presley wasn't done. "And then walk away from the son of a bitch with the matches. I never pictured you for a coward, Dix. I hate to think I have to now."

I let the words sink in. All of them. That last part stung more than it should. I did not want this strong and wonderful lady to see me as a coward. I had way too much respect for her. Admiration.

"So what you're telling me, basically, is not to let the past dictate my future."

"No, Dix." She shook her head. "I'm telling you to grow a pair! Get it? Grow a pair to go with that dick." Mrs. Presley dissolved into another giggling fit.

Great. Just great. My worst nightmare.

I walked to the window. Just in time, as it turned out.

Dylan was out there in the yard talking to Elizabeth. He looked up and his eyes met mine. He signaled me to come down.

"I've got to scoot," I said.

"Thanks for the laughs, Dix. You know I only want the

best for you. I only give you a hard time when you need it."

So much for the sweet old lady.

"Thanks, Mrs. P."

"Oh, and Dix?"

"Yes?"

"I can't wait to tell Craig and Cal about your penis collection."

CHAPTER 9

I DRESSED QUICKLY. Then, as quietly as I could, I scooted down the stairs and out the front door into the cold morning.

I stepped back in again, hopefully quickly enough. Tammy was driving away in her Lexus.

I waited a minute to be sure she was well clear of the yard and then dashed back outside. Elizabeth and Dylan emerged from behind some tarped-up shrubbery where they must have dived to escape Tammy's notice. I jogged over to them.

"Early morning for Tams," I said.

"She doesn't like to be called that," Elizabeth said. "She's probably heading in to the hospital. They often call her in for emergencies."

Well that was odd. Not that Tammy would be needed at the hospital early in the morning, but that Elizabeth would be chastising me for calling her Tams.

"She must be good at what she does," I baited.

Elizabeth nodded. "One of the best."

"So where are we headed?" Dylan directed his question at Elizabeth. "You said you'd take us to see the damaged books?"

Of course Dylan had already tapped her for the

information.

"This way."

I looked at Elizabeth's jogging attire. It was practical looking—a plain navy windbreaker layered over what looked like a normal sweat shirt, navy splash pants, and black runners on her feet. No hot pink or neon orange in sight. I guess that surprised me.

I had no doubt I looked nearly as amazing in the grey sweats I'd slept in. Yes, getting dressed quickly for me had meant tossing on my hat and coat and poking my bare feet into my boots.

Then I checked out the landscaping. Yes, those trails around the grounds were more than shovelled out. They weren't just sanded, they were *freshly* sanded. I was sure of it. We Canadians know winter, and we know our sanded surfaces.

"Morris's doing," Elizabeth said, obviously having noticed my scrutiny of the paths. "He takes care of lots of things,"

It wasn't even six o'clock in the morning yet. How early did the guy get up? Or maybe he was one of those mythical creatures who hardly ever sleep. I'd heard of those.

We walked around the side of the ginormous house until we came to a plain, windowless door. Elizabeth rapped on it twice and, without invite or hesitation, pushed it open.

The lights were already on.

"Morris?" she called. "Are you here?"

From somewhere close yet unseen, Morris answered. "I thought you were coming last night—"

He popped out from behind a set of shelves piled high with tools. His mouth snapped immediately shut when he saw us.

And I had to wonder again what it was that had occupied Elizabeth and Morris on the night of the fire. They were certainly on friendly terms.

Morris was wiping his hand on an oil-spotted rag as he walked around the corner. He balled it up in a tight fist when he saw Dylan and me. His face turned three shades of red as he stood there. He jammed the cloth into his pocket quickly, and then looked for all the world like he wished he still had it to twist in his hands.

Ever-friendly, and in complete guy mode, Dylan dove right into the situation. “Nice workshop you’ve got here.” He moved to admire Morris’s handiwork. Specifically, the intricately carved headboard laid out across two workhorses. There was some fine sanding work going on.

"Thank you," Morris said gruffly.

Dylan began plying Morris with questions, and Morris slowly loosened up.

Leave it to Dylan. He was so good with people. Such a natural at making them feel comfortable. A couple of minutes and the two of them had bonded. All they needed was a hockey game, a case of beer, and flannel shirts, and they’d be all set.

Even Elizabeth seemed to be pulled in, listening as the men-folk discussed the finer points of furniture restoration. With everyone’s focus elsewhere, I took the opportunity to scan the workroom. When we’d first stepped inside, I thought the space was small. But that wasn’t the case at all. It was just packed.

Packed? That was an understatement. Hugh Drammen couldn’t have tossed a single piece of furniture out in his entire life. Hoard much?

Even as that thought crossed my mind, another pushed it out. No, it wasn’t a case of simple hoarding. But someone had certainly been an avid collector of old furniture. My bet was on Tracy, Hugh’s late wife. Which perhaps explained why he hadn’t parted with anything.

It wasn’t like the folks from *Antiques Roadshow* would get a raging hard on over every last bit of it, but I was guessing some of it would definitely raise some...eyebrows.

“Is that the Queen Anne everyone was arguing over?” I asked when there was a lull in the hand-sanding-versus-a-finishing-sander debate. I was pointing to an obvious work in progress standing in the center of a tarpaulin that had been carefully spread on the concrete floor.

Morris looked at me in that is-she-for-real way. "No, that's an ottoman. The Queen Anne is a desk. It right over—"

Elizabeth snapped, "It's not important right now."

I caught that. Whoa! Did I ever. There'd been a hasty visual exchange between Elizabeth and Morris. One that said, "Shut up."

"Morris," Elizabeth said. "My mother and Magnus wanted to see the books that were damaged in the fire."

"Oh, right. I'll just fetch them."

Morris disappeared behind a packed-full shelving unit. A second later, he returned with a grey plastic bin about the size of a laundry basket.

He nodded to a nearby workbench. "Can you get that for me, bud?" he said to Dylan.

"Sure thing." Dylan cleared a spot on the low bench, moving various small tools, cans of varnish, and other materials.

Elizabeth opened the container's lid. "Hugh wants to get these restored. Thankfully, there were no signed first editions in there. He has a shitload of those in his study. These few were probably the least valuable books in his collection."

Ah, but I wasn't looking for an original J.D. Salinger or Alice Munroe that I remembered from Mr. Patterson's grade eleven English Lit. Class. I was looking for clues.

Clues I would find. I was sure of it. Why was I so sure?

'Cause I'm Dix Dodd, that's why.

And in a moment of deserved—and familiar—indulgence, I could practically see the sash emblazoned with the word HERO falling from shoulder to hip across my chest. I could practically feel the hot pink cape billowing out behind me.

Yes, I was, Dix Dodd. If anyone could find evidence, it was—

"I found something," Dylan said.

"Dammit!"

Poof! So much for Dix Dodd, hero. There went my sash and cape.

Dylan narrowed his eyes. “Were you thinking about that sash and cape thing again?”

“Sash and cape thing?” Elizabeth asked. “I take it that’s some kind of sex game?”

I started to shake my head but stopped myself. There was that time on the rooftop…

I shook the image away. “What did you find, Magnus?”

My question had the desired effect of directing everyone’s attention back to Dylan.

“See for yourself,” he challenged. “If you can.”

“You know I can.”

“Bet you can’t.” He closed the book. Closed it and held it out to me. Oh, I got it. Smart-assed, competitive-to-a-fault Dylan Foreman wanted to see if I could spot whatever it was he had spotted.

How childish could he be?

“Usual wager?” I asked, raising a provocative eyebrow.

“Holy shit!” Morris said, suddenly. “Did you know that twitch thing goes all the way to your eyebrow?”

I ignored Morris and just concentrated on Dylan’s smiling face. He nodded, taking me up on that bet.

“Come on, you two, what’s going on?” Elizabeth asked, but I noticed she didn’t say it with much steam. No giving us hell for playing on her dime. She could only play along.

I looked at the book. *Law in the Making* by Carleton Kemp Allen. I flipped it open to the title page. Nope, not signed. Copyright 1927. The book wasn’t in great shape. The fire had wrecked it, but it almost looked like it hadn’t been in great condition before the flames burned off the old, tattered spine. What remained of the pages was brittle, as could be expected, but they also looked like many of them had been dog-eared, especially at the bottom. All in all, it didn’t look like much of a keeper. Was that what Dylan had seen?

“Petty old book, huh?” I said.

Dylan chuckled. "Is that all you got?"

It sure as hell wouldn't be now.

"Of course not," I said.

I opened the volume, started flipping through the pages. I stopped suddenly, close to the middle. Okay, now I saw it. A small, charred, thin stick of wood that could only be —

"It's a match," he said, before I could get the words out.

"Stop stealing my thunder! Of course it's a match."

"What does this mean?" Morris said.

"It means I won the bet." I looked at Dylan. "And I'll be stopping by the cleaners on our way back to the city, to pick up my sash and—"

"About the fire, *Mom*!" Elizabeth said. "What does it tell us about the fire?"

"Right," I said. "It tells us that fire was deliberately set."

Morris shifted on his feet. "Do you think that Uncle Hugh—"

"Not a bloody chance!" Elizabeth looked at Dylan and me fiercely. "No way did Hugh do this. Arson? Why? Hugh-Bear has plenty of money—he's the major stockholder in all the Drammen Industries. And that's the way it stays as long as he's alive. And don't even suggest that he's senile! He's as sane as the day he married me."

The day he married her? Some people might question the sanity of that move.

"Well, Elizabeth," Morris said. "If not Hugh, then who?

Elizabeth scowled at me. Yes, that was for me to find out.

Problem was, I didn't know who either.

CHAPTER 10

ELIZABETH WALKED me outside, closing the workroom door behind us. She not only wanted to rake me over the coals for the lack of progress on the case, she also wanted to make sure I knew that we were expected at dinner that night. All of us.

"Hugh's looking forward to the gathering," she said.

"Really?"

"Really," Elizabeth said. "And do you think you could get that grandmother-from-hell to back off with the whole Elizabeth-Boo-Boo thing. It's not funny."

"No, it's not."

"Then stop laughing, Dix Dodd. Hugh wants to show his in-laws some genuine hospitality. Family hospitality."

Family hospitality? Obviously Hugh hadn't told his young bride he knew who I was. Interesting.

One more thing was discussed before Elizabeth and I parted company: we would keep the discovery of the burned match in the book under wraps. She assured me she'd speak to Morris.

"Don't worry," she said. "He won't say anything." She started off on her overdue jog.

So Dylan and I had the morning to snoop around. I knew he'd hang out with Morris for a while. Under the guise of talking shop, he would check Morris out. He'd also be firing up his laptop to find out what Elizabeth had meant about Hugh being the "major shareholder." Hmm, who else had shares?

As for me, I would have the pleasure of chatting up the martini man himself, Allen Boyden.

I figured the gin and vermouth would cause him to sleep in, so I headed back to the bedroom I was sharing with Mrs. Presley. I prepared myself for the onslaught of pee jokes. But instead I opened the door to find the beds made up, curtains pulled back, and the room perfectly tidied.

And company.

Caryn, who'd seen our bedroom light on in the hallway, had come to check if we needed anything. Mrs. P had promptly advised that I'd take an early-morning stroll—to my boyfriend's room, she suspected. Oh and Mrs. Presley also told Caryn she was going to demonstrate how to make her fabulous pumpkin pancakes for breakfast. Pumpkin pancakes for everyone. Score! They were awesome.

"Then Caryn and I are going to see if we can get the TV bingo channel in the viewing room," Mrs. P said. "That's where they keep their TV."

Caryn smiled. "It's a big screen. A really big screen."

"Wouldn't that be great, D?" Mrs. P said. "If I could play bingo on a great big screen tonight."

"Sounds like a blast."

Caryn and Mrs. P left, presumably for the pumpkin pancake tutorial, and I was finally alone.

So...what to do?

Exactly what I'd been dying to do since the night before—call Rochelle and get the details on her boyfriend, a.k.a. Detective Richard Head. Yes, I'd been trying to do that for a while, with limited success. But lately, there'd been a little give in the dish-the-dirt department. And I wasn't disinclined to use my skills. Stealth, baby. Oh yeah.

I grabbed my cell, hit number four on the speed dial and lay back on the bed as it rang.

"'Lo."

Nice. She answered groggily, which set me up perfectly to say, "You sound tired. Did you have a late one?"

Hee hee hee—Rochelle didn't realize it was such a loaded question.

Say YES for: I had sex last night. NO for: I didn't get lucky.

"What time is it?" she asked.

Damn. Answered with a question!

So what's my obsession on knowing about Rochelle and Richard's love life, you ask? Well, because Rochelle has never told me anything about how they play. Not a blessed word! How unfair is that?

Okay, true, I never had a history with any of Rochelle's previous boyfriends, while I did with Richard. Maybe that was the sticky point.

And before you leap to conclusions, the history Dickhead and I shared was not a romantic one. We had more of an evil nemesis vibe happening.

But that was then. We'd called a truce, unofficial as it was. Okay, make that a quasi-truce. There was still a tension between us, but it stopped short of hostility. An awkwardness but I wasn't really sure why. There was a different quality to it that I just couldn't put my finger on.

"Dix?"

"Huh?"

"I asked what time it is."

I looked at my watch. "Just after six," I said. "So, is that *what time is it* as in *I need more sleep?* Or as is it more of a *why are you calling me at this hour?*"

There was a pause. Her pause.

"You just want to know if Richard and I had sex last night or not. How many times, and how good it was."

I sighed deeply. "Rochelle, I am wounded. Just...wounded. I'd never snoop like that." I contemplated faking an offended sniffle. Except this was me, and she'd never believe it.

"Cut the crap, Dix. Is that the only reason you called—to see if I banged Richard last night?"

Sniffle sniffle "No."

"Dix," Rochelle groaned. "I know you're not really crying. But okay, okay. You woke me up. I could have used more sleep."

I jumped up onto my knees. "How much more sleep?"

"Oh God, Dix, I had sex with Richard. There. Are you satisfied?"

"Are you? Were you?"

She caught my drift.

"Dix, you seem awfully interested in how good my boyfriend is in bed."

Not many things shut me up—that almost did. "That's not it," I finally said. "It's just that you've never held out on me before. And you know me—the less you say, the more I want to know."

Rochelle let out a deep sigh of her own. And she was not faking it. "Okay, you win."

I perked up. "I do?"

"Sex with Richard is a little like being captured by a caveman."

My eyes widened. "You mean wham, bam, and it's over."

"God, no. But it's a little...animalistic. Like a force of nature, you know? A wild, pounding force of nature."

No. I did not know. Not that I had any complaints with Dylan. Nada. He had humor, finesse, unstoppable goodness, and what was that other thing. Ah, yes, a huge dong. But Richard? A primal force of nature?

She sighed. "Even the way he looks at me. I feel a bit like prey when that light comes into his eyes. It's just fierce and raw and wanton and...primal."

That shut me up.

"Satisfied?"

I shook my head, dislodging the mind pictures. "Well, not that I was over curious."

She snorted and started giving me more details. No, not of the sex life she shared with Richard Head but the other day-to-day stuff going on with her. The Judge was away all that week, so Rochelle was looking forward to a slower day at work. She was meeting her sister, Tatum, for lunch. She'd gotten that leather jacket we'd seen last week at the West Marport Mall.

And I'm sorry to say I tuned her out. I didn't mean to, but my mind had drifted elsewhere. Fierce. Raw. Primal. Animalistic.

What would that be like?

CHAPTER 11

AFTER HANGING UP with Rochelle, I hit the shower.

I couldn't stop thinking about what Rochelle had said. Sex with Richard was...what was that word?

Animalistic.

Right. That was the—*soapy suds, warm water sliding lower and lower...ah, that's the spot*—word.

Curse you, detachable shower head! Who the heck had time for this?

Apparently, I did.

How primal was she talking about?

Ten minutes later, I towelled my waterlogged skin with the most impossibly soft towel and wrapped said fluffy towel around myself. Then I grabbed a hand towel and swiped off the bathroom mirror to see my smiling self. Strangely smiling self.

Ah, satisfaction in the shower. In a strange house, which naturally only made it better. But where had that sudden urge come from? There was a full length mirror attached to the back of the bathroom door. I glanced at the pushed-back shower curtain behind me. Yeah, I blamed the shower. The soft, warm water. The steam.

Ah, who was I kidding? It had me at detachable shower head.

Hmmmmmm...head.

Head?

Head!

Oh my freakin' God! I'd just gotten off thinking about Richard Head!

"Can I help you?"

I'd been standing in the Drammen kitchen, staring out a window, desperately searching the winter-grey sky. I turned to face the owner of the voice, a young lady in an apron. She must be part of the day staff.

"Caryn told me we had company," the woman said. Then, picking up on the shell-shocked expression I was no doubt wearing, her forehead creased with concern. "Are you all right, Ms. Bee? Is there anything I can help you with?"

"Could you...could you take a look out the window?" I gestured behind me to indicate the winter wonderland outside.

Her eyes widened. "Why?"

"I want you to tell me if you see any pigs flying around out there?"

And please say yes! The day I entertained sexual fantasies about Richard-freakin'-Head was the day pigs would fly, surely.

Frown deepening, she looked out the window. "Oh, yes." Her voice wobbled with uncertainty. "Um...there's one up over the willow tree. Flying right over. And it's...it's waving at you." She gave a little wave with her hand toward the glass. Then she turned to me and asked nervously, "Do you see it too?"

I think she meant, *Do you see it, bat-shit crazy lady?*

I drew a deep breath and exhaled it on a sigh. "No. But thanks for being so kind."

"Oh, thank God! Caryn told me Elizabeth's family was a little odd. I was afraid you were—"

Her mouth snapped closed.

"No worries," I said, extending my hand. "And please, call me D. I'm Elizabeth's mother."

"I'm Glori." She shook my hand. "You had me a little worried there!" She smiled shyly. "I'll get your breakfast for you, if that's all right?"

"Yes, please."

"Okay," she said. But Glori was clearly talking to herself, not me. It was more of a ready-set-go or possibly a what-first kind of okay.

"I think my mother was making pancakes," I said.

"Right!" Glori's face brightened. "They're warming in the oven still. Would you like butter? Molasses?"

"Got any maple syrup?" I asked hopefuly.

"I think we have some." She turned to the cupboard then back around quickly. "I'll just set you a place in the dining room first."

"If it's all right, Glori, I'll sit here with you."

She seemed suddenly more flustered, as if wondering if it was indeed all right. That was all I needed to confirm my initial hunch: Glori was new.

I didn't wait for an answer but sat myself down on a kitchen stool. Glori seemed relieved she didn't have to make a decision. She crossed the kitchen, opened the oven door, and pulled out a warming plate with a high stack of pumpkin pancakes. Oh yum. Mrs. P had made enough to feed a couple of hungry lumberjacks. Or me.

Glori brought me the butter in a fancy glass dish. "Now, where do we keep the syrup?"

"In the cupboard?" I guessed.

"Lois told me where, but she's off this morning. I wonder…" She snapped her fingers. "Oh right!"

The young lady knelt down to the bottom cupboard, and she did so with nary a creak or pop of her joints. I vaguely remember what that was like. She dug around a minute before coming up with a small bottle of pure maple syrup—maple leaf-shaped and everything.

"I didn't mean to put you to so much trouble," I said.

"No problem." She started to turn. "Lois looks after the kitchen—she knows exactly where everything is. This is actually only the third time I've taken care of things by myself. But she had a mammogram scheduled for this morning."

"Nothing wrong, I hope."

"Just routine."

"So, tell me about yourself, Glori," I said as I slathered on the butter and poured on a generous amount of that maple goodness. "Have you been with the Drammen family for long?"

"Not long." She shook her head. "Just short of three months."

Hmm, we were looking at November again. Busy month.

"Do you like it here?"

Glori lit right up. "I love it," she said. "I was so lucky to get this job."

"Lucky, why?"

She shrugged. "Let's just say I've...I've had my ups and downs." Her right hand went to her left arm, as if to scratch an imaginary itch.

"Everything's going well now, I hope."

"They are now, but things haven't always been so good."

I lifted an inquiring eyebrow.

She bit her lip. "Those pigs you were asking about? I've seen them a time or two myself, if you know what I mean. In fact, I wasn't just seeing them; I was flying right along beside them."

Drugs. It had to be. We probably weren't talking marijuana. "Good for you for getting it all straightened out," I said, meaning it.

She looked up, meeting my eyes. I was struck by the

dignity I saw there.

"I've been clean since September twenty-third when I checked myself into rehab. Completely. It was hard for a couple days when I first got out, but I must have had an angel on my shoulder or something. I was thankful to get this job. I...I don't know what I'd be doing now if I hadn't. It's the first legit one I've had."

I appreciated Glori's honesty. Admired her fortitude. Her strength. Her determination to turn her life around.

But that was women for you.

And I liked Glori even more as she put a cup of steaming hot coffee in front of me.

While I ate the world's most delicious pancakes, Glori busied herself around the kitchen. And we chatted. Not so much about me but about her. I think it was easier for her to talk about that stuff while her hands were busy doing something else. Had she been sitting across the table from me, she might not have spoken so frankly about her life in Toronto and the home she'd run away from. The clean friends she was beginning to make. It was an easy conversation and easier with every passing moment. She was certainly fond of the Drammens. Well, all but one.

"Would you mind if I took this with me?" I pointed to the steaming cup. It was one of those wide-handled jobbies, and it fit so cozily in my hand. It was also very large and full of...*ahhhh*...Colombian dark roast.

"Not at all," Glori said.

"I think I'll go for a walk," I said. "See who's around. Maybe I'll bump into Allen."

The mood changed just that quickly. It was like a cold cloud suddenly descended over the sunny kitchen.

"Oh," Glori said. "Um, I could get fired over this, but just so you know, Allen is...."

"An asshole."

"Yeah. Watch out for him."

"Why?"

She shook her head. "Just do."

"Any particular reason?"

"I guess he didn't always used to be such a jerk. Was nice, even, according to Lois. But he changed just before I got here."

She crossed her arms around herself, in that protective mode. Could that mean she meant *jerk* in the sense I thought she did? If so, some real ass-kicking might yet be in order.

"Glori, do you mean jerk as in…"

She shook her head. "He tried to get friendly with me one time, right in front of his wife! But I set him straight."

"Good."

"Did you tell Hugh or Elizabeth?"

"No, but I did tell Caryn. She said she'd take care of it, and he hasn't bothered me since." Glori picked up my syrup-sticky plate. "It was nice meeting you, D. I'd better get back to work. Watch out for the pigs."

"The flying ones?"

"Them too." She smiled, topped off my coffee, and turned back to her kitchen chores.

I found the pig...er, Allen in the parlor. That was where the bar was, so it was the first place I looked. But, he wasn't sucking back green olives or sipping away on a drink yet. The curtains were pulled closed, and I almost didn't see him in the dimly lit room. He was reclining on the long sofa where Dylan, Mrs. Presley, and I had sat the night before. Allen lay there with a hand over his eyes. He was business-suit dressed, right down to the shiny black shoes which rested on the cushions. He looked like he needed the peace and quiet the dark room offered. Yeah, even with his face half covered I could see it—the guy oozed hungover.

So I set my voice to shrill and opened my mouth to shout, "Wake up!" but then a cell phone rang. Allen's cell phone. He dug it out of his pocket, and I stepped out of the doorway to listen.

"Dammit, Bean. You were supposed to call last night! What the hell happened? Tammy's starting to suspect I'm lying… No more excuses. I'm paying you very well to get this done. Now, get that picture!"

He put the phone away.

Bean?

Bean Jones? It had to be. It's not a name you hear every day.

Bean Jones was to me as Moriarti was to Sherlock Holmes. Tall, bald, knuckle-cracking, whiskey-drinking, woman-hating jerk. Also the big boss at Jones and Associates.

Huh, Allen had Bean himself working for him? Not one of his minions? Allen must be paying high dollar indeed.

Get that picture! That's what he had ordered.

Holy crap. What picture were they discussing? In my line of work, a picture someone wanted found that desperately almost always meant the subject parties were in a—cough cough—compromising position.

Footsteps.

Allen was on his feet in the parlor, beginning to pace. I waited a full minute, before I quickly walked into the room. "Oh, Allen," I said, stopping short just inside the doorway. "I didn't know you were in here."

He managed a pasty smile. Those olives were affecting his skin tone. "Sure you didn't, baby. You know you want a piece of this."

This?

I looked around for cake. Nope. He had meant himself.

What I wanted was to puke. The guy was a genuine sleaze. But I genuinely needed some information from him. So should I flirt? Batting my eyelashes was definitely out of the question. Could I do something sexy/slutty, something in line with my D Bee rep? Hmm, I'd seen Miley doing that twerking thing…

What the hell.

Legs apart, elbows out, waist bent, I contorted into position. Christ, Mother had told me how natural it felt—was she ever wrong.

"Watch your back," Allen said. Clearly he wasn't getting turned on here. Just that quickly, he'd backed off. Pulled away. No more cheap lines or sleazy come-ons.

I straightened. Hmmm, that was interesting.

It was as if he had been yanked back by a chain. Allen Boyden was a man of all talk and truly no action. At least with me… Maybe he had himself a mistress on the side? Were they—Allen and the unknown woman—the subject of said pictures? Was someone blackmailing him?

Choosing a chair built for one, I sat down by the fireplace. Allen resettled on the sofa.

"So, what's got you up so early in the morning?" he asked.

"I always wake up early," I said. "And I'm bored. I can only take so much of my mother."

"Where's your boyfriend?"

"Magnus is off somewhere with Morris."

"Let me guess—skinning beavers? Wrestling elk? Or building some sort of...wood thing?"

Yeah, I had a real man's man sitting there with me. *Not.*

"Something like that. Magnus has his assets," I said, positively purring the words, "but occasionally, I like the company of a more...civilized man."

"Is that...I think you've got spittle on your chin."

Crap!

"Whoops!" I dabbed my chin as delicately as I could with my sleeve. So much for the sexy purring. Maybe I'd try a more direct approach. "So, Allen, tell me about yourself."

His eyes narrowed. "Why?"

"Just curious. How did you end up here?"

"You mean with the Drammens."

I nodded.

"I married Tammy."

Well, duh. I forced my lips into a smile. "How did you two

meet?"

"You really want to know this?"

"Oh, I'm a hopeless romantic."

He eyed me. "Bull puckey. You're just nosy."

I laughed. "Busted."

He laughed too. Good.

Allen drew a deep breath, the first semi-relaxed one I'd seen him take. "Tammy and I met through friends of friends when she was just out of med school. I was working at Baytona-Bash insurance back then."

"Doing what?"

"Same as I do now. Sales. But that was the late eighties. Things have changed in the industry."

Had they ever.

"But some things stay the same," I offered. "You two are still together."

That olive-green cast to his complexion deepened. "We're holding on," he said. "Well, at least one of us is." He got to his feet and started pacing again. "I'd rather not talk about my marriage."

"Sorry," I lied. "Didn't mean to get personal. I wasn't trying to pry. I have such a hard time sticking to just one guy. I admire a couple who sticks together especially in this day and age when so much can rip them apart. Money problems…"

No response.

"Differences in child rearing…"

That received more of a tensing of posture, a flicker of a misstep. Not much, but noticeable to one who really watched.

Then I went in for the kill. I lowered my tone so he'd have to reach for the words. "Infidelity, even."

Allen whirled on me. "What did you say?"

"Infidelity. You know, hanky panky. Bumping uglies."

Allen looked like he wanted to simultaneously cry and rip my head off. (I'd say about fifty-five/forty-five for the ripping; I have experience in this area.)

“What?” Allen’s voice rose. “What do you mean by that?”

I shrugged. “It happens with lots of marriages.”

“Not with this marriage!”

“Come on, Allen. Surely you’ve slid your portfolio into someone else’s...um...horizontal filing cabinet.”

“What? That’s the—”

"Truth?"

“Hell, no. I was going to say that’s the worst bloody metaphor I’ve ever heard.”

Not what I’d been going for.

“And I told you, I don’t want to talk about my marriage.” He glanced at his watch. “I’ve got to get going. I can’t be late this—”

“So, crazy about that fire in your father-in-law’s study the other night,” I said. “Elizabeth was telling me about it.”

He rolled his eyes and headed for the wet bar. “Crazy about everything around here. But yes, that was strange.”

“Little early for a drink, isn’t it?”

He stood before the bar like a man who was definitely on familiar territory, but when he spoke, he said, “It’s not a drink I’m after.”

He crouched down, and after a quick look around to make sure no one other than me was there, he opened the left-hand panel. Then he reached inside—way inside—and pulled something out.

I pushed back in the chair. A gun? A knife? Something to tame that horrible cowlick of his?

None of the above. Allen pulled out a pack of cigarettes.

“I thought Hugh didn’t allow smoking in the house?”

“He doesn’t.”Allen stood. “The old man doesn’t know I smoke. As far as everyone here knows, I quit two years ago. I smoke when they’re not around, in the car on my way to work. Once in a while in the house if I’m sure I’ll be alone for a bit. I trust you not to say anything, D.” He pocketed the smokes and buttoned his suit jacket.

I stopped him just before he left the room. “What about the

fire? What do you think happened?"

He sneered at me. Or rather he sneered at the question. "What do I think happened?"

I nodded.

"I think people in this house have an awful habit of pretending to be one thing and being another. Lying about their whereabouts."

"Whereabouts...on the night of the fire?"

"I've got to go. See you at dinner, D, and don't be late," he said as he walked away. "Hugh likes to pretend."

"Pretend what?"

He turned quickly. Quickly enough that he didn't get a chance to hide the sneer. "Just know this: things aren't what they seem."

Well, well. Lots to think about. Allen's parting words. The phone call with Bean and the mysterious picture. And last but not least, the other item he'd pulled out of that hiding place in the bar along with that twenty-five-pack of Players Rich cigarettes.

A box of wooden matches.

CHAPTER 12

THE REST OF the day was quiet. Frustratingly so. Why, it was enough to make a person want to take another shower.

But four in one day is too much for anyone.

As the clock ticked on, more and more it looked like we'd be spending another night as guests of the Drammens.

How had I spent my valuable time that day?

I'd wandered around the house checking things out. No, I wasn't turning over mattresses or fluffing up pillows (I always thought I'd make a wonderful fluffer). I wasn't dusting around for fingerprints. I wasn't checking behind sofa cushions for loose change or hidden cell phones. I was feeling my way around the Drammen home for my intuition to kick in.

Kick in?

Make that a flying, leaping, dropkick in.

Lately, my intuition had powered up a notch. Those niggles and nudges more and more turned out to be full-on body slams. My intuitive skills were growing. No question about it.

But did I get that full Kung-Fu treatment as I wandered the house? Not a bit of it. Nothing.

At least not initially.

So how did luxury-loving Mrs. Presley feel about another night away from her precious sons? Well, pretty damned all right.

And get this—Mrs. P was going to get to break out those colorful dabbers and even more colorful troll dolls she'd packed after all. She'd roped Tammy into picking up TV bingo cards. She'd found her number programmed into the house phones and called her. Tammy—presumably because she was too stunned by the request to deny it—had agreed to buy them. I could just imagine Tammy's disbelief as Mrs. P placed her order and advised which convenience stores would be most likely to carry the cards.

I didn't see Hugh at all during the day. Nor did I see any more of Elizabeth. After her delayed morning jog, she'd spent the rest of the morning with her husband while he worked. Yes, *worked*. I found out—thank you Glori, once again, for being just as chatty when I returned the coffee mug—that once seven twenty-five rolled around, Hugh and Humphrey shut themselves up in Hugh's office for the rest of the morning. While the study's door was always open, according to Glori, Hugh's office definitely was not.

At seven thirty exactly, Hugh's breakfast was to be placed on a tray and taken to him in his office. It was the same meal every day—black coffee, the fresh-squeezed juice of two oranges, two cream cheese danishes warmed in the microwave for exactly forty-three seconds, two slices of turkey bacon, and two turkey breakfast sausages. It was a pretty safe bet that half of that grub was for Humphrey.

Glori further told me that Elizabeth insisted on delivering the tray herself. But Elizabeth's solicitude didn't stop there. She didn't drop off the tray and leave to pursue her own distractions. She actually stayed with the old guy while he worked, which he did right up until twelve noon, when he finished up just in time for lunch.

I wasn't at all surprised to learn that Hugh still managed the family business. Obviously he had underlings to look after the individual properties and such, but when it came to the high level stuff, the old guy still kept a very close eye on the family fortune. I had every confidence he kept everything humming right along.

And Elizabeth probably made sure other things were humming right along too. And she could keep a close eye on her DON'T-YOU-DARE-DIE hubby, as well as a sly eye on the rest of the family assets. Elizabeth Bee-Drammen never missed a trick.

Good for her.

So yeah, as far as the investigation went, it was a pretty uneventful day. Yes, we now knew the fire had been the result of arson, but I was no closer to knowing who struck that match we'd found.

But remember how my intuition had been jumping lately? Well, it sure ramped up later in the day, when I heard Dylan whispering into his cell phone.

Or was I being paranoid?

I caught up with Dylan as he was lurking outside Hugh's study. And no, I don't mean lurking in that good and totally justifiable PI way. I knew it the instant I saw him glancing quickly around to see if anyone was there before he answered his cell. That *anyone* in this particular instance included me.

I froze.

Dylan's back was to me. He didn't see me as he stepped into the study. He pulled the door behind him but didn't latch it shut. It was obvious he wanted privacy for his call.

Did I give it to him?

Hell, no. I crept up to the door and stood just outside to listen in.

"Hey," he said. "Glad you called." He did sound glad.

"Oh yeah, it will be a good weekend."

So he was talking to one of the law school friends about the camping trip. I heard the string of "Right...beer...sure we'll have a bonfire. Sounds great. Yeah, looking forward to see you too."

And on that latter line, my ears perked up. Which was silly. It was just one of the law school pals. Just Jack or Chevy or—

"Been a long time, Saffron."

My heart leapt in the pause, as Dylan listened.

"I can't believe you kept that!" he said. "God, yes. That was a wild, huh? Your father looked like he wanted to carve me up along with the turkey." He laughed. "Ah, good times, huh?"

Saffron. He'd met her folks. And turkey? Obviously they'd spent a holiday together. And his voice had gone down when he'd said her name. That pretty damned name. Not in a way that anyone else would notice, but I listened on a different level.

So why had he gone into hiding when the phone rang? Was it because he didn't want to jeopardize his cover? Didn't want a member of the Drammen household to overhear him talking to a female other than his sugar mama, D?

Or was it because he didn't want *me* to overhear him talking to her?

Probably both.

"Later, gator," Dylan said, obviously concluding the call.

I silently counted to ten and then walked briskly into the room as though I'd been hurrying down the hall, not standing right outside the door eavesdropping.

The curtains were pulled wide; light streamed in the window. Nobody was trying to catch anyone doing anything unaware in the dark. But had I caught him just the same? Maybe I was just being paranoid.

"Hey," I prompted. "Anything new?"

Or, more specifically, anything you'd like to tell me about?

Dylan answered quickly. "I had an interesting talk with Morris today."

"Yeah?"

"Yeah. Once he got going, I couldn't shut him up. He's starting to miss the North. Looking to leave soon. Get back to his old work in Alaska."

"Back to work? So Hugh's not paying him?"

Dylan shook his head. "Oh, Hugh's paying him all right. Very well, in fact. He's even offered to move Morris down here permanently. But money doesn't seem to be the highest priority for this guy."

"He told you all this?" I asked.

He grinned. "Yes. And I verified the money part. Hugh may run the company, but Morris holds thirty percent of the shares, left to him by his father, Prosser Drammen. Hugh owns the rest of them."

Hmmmm, that was interesting.

"Nice work," I said.

He shrugged. "I fired up my laptop, made some inquiries, got some answers."

"Do you think he'll go back to Alaska soon?"

"Probably. You can see how painful it is for him to interact with people. He's definitely an introvert."

"I'll say."

"But he's happily introverted, you know? Likes his own company."

"And likes the world to leave him alone?"

"Pretty much. He spends most of his time here in that little shop. He's quite the master craftsman, really."

I frowned. "Wonder what's keeping him here?"

"He's the kind of guy who won't leave until the job is done."

"So, he's going to stay until every bit of furniture in that workshop is redone? That'll take years."

"Not quite," Dylan said. "He's going to stay until the most valuable and important pieces are done. There's a couple left."

It didn't take a shitload of intuition to guess what one of those pieces was. "The Queen Anne desk that Elizabeth and Tammy were fighting over?"

"That is one fantastic item," he said. "Seriously, Dix. I've never seen a piece of furniture like it."

I listened as Dylan elaborated. And yes, held my tongue. Was he going to tell me about Saffron? Or not? And just what was I going to do about that?

CHAPTER 13

I ALMOST FELT BAD that I wouldn't be there to see the Queen Anne when it was done. Not that I'm into antiques. My living room has a few retro-eighties pieces, including a set of nice red-shaded, standing lamps. I got them from Mrs. Presley about a year ago when she renovated the Underwood for the first time since she'd bought the place. The woman does buy quality.

But the Queen Anne desk sounded incredibly intriguing to me, especially as Dylan elaborated on the work Morris was doing. Hidden compartments? False-bottom drawers? We were talking a PI's dream here. Wow, the secrets a desk like that could hold. Evidence. Weapons... Like a gun. Or a knife. A carving knife. A turkey carving knife…

Dammit.

"So, what do you think, Dix?" My mind had been drifting, but Dylan's words pulled me back.

"Huh?"

"What do you think about this whole investigation? About the match we found in that old law book? Matches don't ignite on their own."

"No, they don't. Nor do mats come unglued." I crouched

down to the mat at my feet—the one Hugh had gone sliding on—which had since dried and been put back in place. I flipped it over. I set it down again and stood.

"Rubber rings all glued on," I said. "Hugh won't be doing a downward facing anything tonight!"

Dylan's eyes widened.

What? All I'd said was...

Ah, context! I hadn't told him about my earlier musings of Hugh doing yoga over Elizabeth's ampleness.

"Yoga, Dylan! Yoga. Yesterday it looked like Hugh was doing yoga over Elizabeth, so I was thinking—oh, never mind."

"What any two people do in the privacy of their own bedroom is their business, Dix."

"Oh, really? Tell that to my blog!"

Dylan shook his head. "About the fire…"

Yeah, definitely time to get back on topic.

"Someone had to have set it," I said. "And I'm guessing it was the same someone who wanted Hugh to take a tumble on this mat."

"We've got the match. But why would someone light a match and shove it into a book?"

I didn't have an answer. "I saw Allen with a box of wooden matches earlier," I said, adding yet another piece to the puzzle.

"Right. But anyone could get matches. It's not like we're dealing with a bunch of school kids here."

"Speaking of school kids," I said. "What the hell is up with Roma? Why was she in here?"

We both glanced at the beautiful mahogany desk. Simultaneously, we nodded.

"Yeah," I said. "We totally did it under there last night."

He hesitated. "That's just what I was thinking."

No chance in hell was that what he'd been thinking.

Dylan walked quickly behind the desk. The top drawer—the one that Roma had been going through—was unlocked.

I listened at the door as Dylan rifled through the papers. One unsealed envelope in particular seemed to catch his attention. He held it up. "It's from Marport U."

"What is it?"

Dylan peered inside the envelope. "It's a check. It looks to be a refund on Roma's tuition." Dylan looked up at me. He started to say something but then stopped. Because he heard the same thing I did—footsteps in the hallway.

Shit! Someone was coming.

"Don't even think it," I whispered as Dylan glanced toward the desk. "Unless you were thinking about some more elevator-type—"

He rolled his eyes. Then he grabbed a book. Good idea. I pulled one off the shelf too, just in time as Caryn walked into the room.

"Oh, there you are," she said. "I'm surprised to find you here."

"I hope it's all right?" I said. "We were bored so thought we'd come find a little light reading. Elizabeth said to make ourselves at home."

"Of course." Caryn smiled, but tightly as she looked over at the book in my hand. "What are you reading?"

Good question.

I looked down at the title.

Light reading, my ass…

"A Preliminary Survey of the Law of Real Property," I said.

Crap.

I faked as much interest as I could. "It's by—"

"Cornelius J. Moynihan," Caryn said. "1940, West Publishing Company. One hundred and fifty four pages, including a sizeable index."

I checked it out. "You're right."

Caryn smiled broadly.

"You've read it?" Dylan asked.

She shook her head. "No. But I've kept house for Hugh for

so long, I've flipped through more than a few of them. Hugh collects books like his late wife collected antiques. Tracy liked old furniture. Hugh likes old books."

"How about Hugh? Has he read all these books?" He reshelved the tome he'd been holding.

Caryn walked over to where Dylan was standing and gently eased the book he'd replaced out again. She ran her fingertips along the book's spine and reshelved it. Only then did she answer Dylan's question. "Hugh's not an educated man in the formal sense, but he's smart as they come. And yes, he's read every book in this collection."

I was next. Caryn took the law book from my hands (and I was just about to get to the good part!). She slid that one back into place too. Slowly.

Perfectly.

"I could have put that back," I said.

"Ah, but I know just how Hugh likes them arranged. He's very picky about his books." Caryn did a visual inspection of the room. Twice around. Finally, she said. "Hugh wants us all to meet in the parlor before dinner."

"What time?" Dylan asked.

"Five o'clock. I know that seems early, but with Tammy's work schedule, we like to eat early around here. And too, that way, Hugh can retire to his study at—"

"Exactly seven o'clock," I said.

Caryn hesitated a moment before she nodded. "If you take any more books off the shelves, just leave them on the desk for me. I'll make sure they're put back right." She turned on her heel and left the study.

"Well, Dix, I guess we should—"

"Can I use your cell?" Expectantly, I held out my hand. "I want to check the office messages."

"Where's yours?"

"Left it in the room."

Liar, liar pants on fire.

No, I wasn't jealous. No, I did not think Dylan was

cheating on me. Hell no. He's a decent guy. But...but I'm not stupid, and I trust my intuition.

Dylan looked at me curiously, but he withdrew the phone from the back pocket of his Magnus-approved butt-hugging jeans. He handed it over, and yes, I did check to see last number called. He'd called it five times before.

I started to hand the phone back.

"Aren't you going to retrieve the messages?" His voice was a flat monotone.

So he knew I'd been snooping. And if he asked me why I was snooping, I could be pretty sure he hadn't been talking to an old girlfriend. On the other hand, if he *didn't* ask why, then he—

"Let me know if there's anything urgent," he said, then walked away, leaving me holding his phone.

Shit.

I dialed in for messages. There were two:

A robo-dialing ship's captain was thrilled to tell me that I'd won that coveted all-inclusive trip for two to some sandy destination. If only I'd just press that number one to be connected to an operator. And oh, have my credit card ready to pay the taxes.

Uh, no.

Secondly: A bank totally not attached to my credit card wanted to do a survey about how happy I was with my credit card.

That was it.

Well, except for that other message I'd got loud and clear from Dylan: he did not want me to know that one of his old, stand-by-me law school buddies had been his girlfriend.

Why the hell hadn't he told me about Saffron? There's a difference between law school buddy and law school buddy-he-was-banging.

Had he loved her?

Whoa. I was *not* jealous. Dix Dodd does not do jealous.

"Thanks," I said, my voice chipper, and handed him back

his phone.

CHAPTER 14

DESPITE MY slightly-less-than-comfortable feelings about Dylan's former romance with Saffron, the first and foremost thing on my mind was the case.

And I did not want the ever-perceptive Mrs. Presley to know anything was amiss. So as I met her back in the room, I made sure to tell her what a kick-ass day I'd had.

"I had a totally kick-ass day, Mrs. P." I shut the door behind me and plunked down on the bed.

She listened and nodded as I elaborated on my visit with Allen and that mysterious phone call. I told her also about the matches he'd grabbed from under the bar and the single match we'd found embedded in the spine of one of the fire-damaged books. I passed on Dylan's intel concerning Morris Drammen. Dished out the information Glori had given me.

And honestly by the time I finished, I was feeling a little bit better. Calmer.

Okay, less jealous.

"Did you want to know what I found out from Caryn?" Mrs. Presley asked.

I nodded. "Gimmee, gimmee, gimmee."

"Nothing. Nada." Mrs. P made a zipping motion across her

lips.

Though information had been fairly easily gotten from Glori, not a peep could be had from the loyal Caryn.

“Family,” Mrs. P said, by way of explanation.

“But Caryn’s not related.”

Mrs. Presley shook her head. “It’s not always about blood. You know better than that, Dix.”

“It’s snowing,” Mrs. Presley said.

She was right. It was coming down like a blanket of white as we entered the parlor and gazed out through the floor to ceiling windows overlooking the snow-covered back yard.

“Guess you’ll need a bigger shovel if you’re going to get that balcony cleared in time for breakfast tomorrow?” she said.

“You’re kidding, right?”

Our conversation ended quickly when we were no longer alone in the parlor.

Unbelievably, Tammy really had stopped by a convenience store and picked up the bingo cards that Mrs. Presley had requested. Which both surprised me and raised her in my estimation.

And she was the first to join us. Unasked, Tammy poured a glass of wine for Mrs. Presley and me, as well as herself. Mrs. P and I were sitting on that long couch again, and she took a chair across from us. Tammy was looking brighter today. Less worn, despite the hours she’d spent in surgery. That is, until her husband walked into the room. Just that quickly, her smile vanished.

And speaking of all things surgical… I had to wonder why the hell Tammy didn’t cut that clown loose. Seriously. Okay, maybe Allen hadn’t always been an asshole, as Glori had said, but he was more than making up for it now. He started in with the flirting again immediately. And yes, I knew it was for

Tammy's benefit, not mine.

"I bet you'd take a pretty picture, D," he said.

Picture? Again with a picture?

Tammy downed her wine in one gulp and went to the bar for another glass.

When she turned away, I narrowed my eyes and looked at Allen and mouthed the words: "I have pepper spray in my purse." I pointed to the small black purse on my lap.

Apparently unfazed, he winked.

Get that picture, Bean! He'd been dead serious when he'd said that. And pictures usually meant hanky-panky. But frankly, I had a hard time imagining that Allen ever got laid. Like, by a real person, breathing and everything. Which made it hard to imagine someone getting a good money shot. But what else could it be?

"I hope everyone's hungry." Elizabeth said brightly as she entered the room. Hugh was at her side, looking dapper in dress pants and a sweater. He looked so...normal and approachable. Sure, the pants were fine worsted wool and the sweater cashmere, but he wore it so comfortably. Morris stood off to the side behind them. He'd traded his tattered working clothes for much snazzier duds. Elizabeth was dressed in a fabulous charcoal pantsuit that managed to look understated—no small feat, considering the lush assets it was covering. Like any good social climber, she'd cultivated good taste.

I wasn't the only one to notice how nicely Elizabeth was turned out.

"Oh, Boo-Boo," Mrs. P said. "Where did you get those earrings?" Drawing everyone's attention to them. Yeah, even mine.

Wow—those were some big diamond studs.

Elizabeth touched a perfectly manicured hand to one ear. "They're new. I ordered them from Tiffany's."

My eyes shot to Tammy to catch her reaction, but she didn't bat an eyelash. Hell, she didn't even look up. She just took another drink of wine.

"They must have cost a pretty penny," Allen sniped.

Hugh abruptly ended that line of questioning. "Not that's it's a concern of yours, Allen."

And for the first time in...well, ever...I saw Morris smile with ease as Hugh put Allen in his place. That smile really made him look attractive. As did his choice of apparel tonight. I recognized it as the outfit he'd worn to the wedding. There was a crisp crease in his pants. His shirt looked freshly pressed, too. He wasn't wearing a tie, but the sports jacket was a good one. And I must admit he looked pretty nice.

But not Dylan-nice. Even though I was still a little miffed with him, I had to admit, he looked positively edible as he strolled into the parlor. He gave manly nods to Hugh and Morris. Then greeted Caryn, Mrs. P, and Tammy. Yes, Dylan Foreman looked like a million bucks. No, wait—make that nine hundred and ninety-nine thousand. One thing was missing... Not that the mustache had been *that* expensive. Damned math again.

"You shaved," Caryn said.

Dylan's fingers shot to his whiskerless upper lip and down again. "Yes," he said. "I thought it was time for a change." He looked at me. "Do you like it, baby?"

He looked at me in that *dammit* way.

I shrugged. It wasn't the end of the world that Dylan had forgotten part of the disguise. I mean, Hugh had already ID'd me as Dix Dodd, Private Eye Extraordinaire (my words, not his, but you know he had to be thinking it). So it was not exactly the greatest leap in logic that he'd also recognized Dylan. And, not for the first time, I wondered how Elizabeth had been so wrong about her husband's observational skills. The guy knew more about what was going on around him than she gave him credit for.

Maybe more than anyone gave him credit for…

"I like it," Mrs. P said. "Makes you look younger. And less like a porn star."

But I liked my boyfriend looking like a porn star.

Mustache or no, Dylan swaggered over in full boy toy mode. He sat down beside me and rested his hand on my knee, giving it a squeeze.

"Beer, Magnus?" Caryn asked.

His decline was timely, as just then, Glori poked her head into the parlor to announce dinner was ready.

Mrs. P was first to her feet.

As the party started to exit the room, Elizabeth latched onto me. "Can I have a word with you, Mother?" She didn't wait for my answer, but looked at Hugh as she pulled me aside. "I'll just be a second, Hugh-Bear. You don't mind, do you?"

"Not at all."

Mrs. P instantly took Dylan's arm. "Lucky you, you get to escort a real lady to the table, Magnus. A good-looking one too."

"Indeed, Nanny Jane," he said.

"I'll walk with you, Dad," Tammy said. She linked her arm in his, and he patted her hand.

Without a word to each other—without so much as a sideways glance—Allen and Morris trailed behind.

Elizabeth kept a smile on her face until everyone had left the room. "Okay, Dodd, what do you know?"

What did I know?

"Well, where shall we start? The indefinite integral of one over x is equal to...twelve."

"That's bullshit," she said. "It's equal to the natural log of the absolute value of x plus a constant! Come on, Dix! Don't play stupid!"

What the hell?

The enigma known as Elizabeth Bee-Drammen deepened.

But wait. Could I use that math aptitude she possessed to my advantage somehow?

"Hey, Elizabeth, you know the whole half-your-age-plus-nine rule...is there a way you could round that up or move a decimal or something?"

"Dix, get serious," she said. "I hired you for two reasons:

to keep my husband safe and to find out who was trying to hurt him. So who is it?"

Dammit. I had no flippant comeback for that. All I could do was give her the truth, unpalatable as it was. "I...I don't know. *Yet*."

"But you will?"

I returned her measuring gaze with a confident one of my own. I nodded. "I will."

As we exited the parlor, I hoped to God I was right. Not for the money. Okay, yes for the money. But it was more than that. All afternoon, a feeling of unease had been closing in on me. Something was up. Something was about to happen.

I just hadn't known how soon it would be.

CHAPTER 15

ELIZABETH AND I plastered on phony smiles as we walked into the dining room.

I thought it would be a good idea to make like we'd just come from a real mother-daughter conversation. Something believable. Like family business. Hometown gossip. Or some sort of obscure but scary as hell medical condition.

Yeah, me—I thought of the perfect thing to say: "So then my doctor said the words *idiopathic nut sack*. Do you think I should get a second opinion?"

"Mother!" Elizabeth gasped. "Now's not the time."

If not now, when? Tammy was a doctor after all. Maybe she could give me some free medical advice. Some reassurance.

Yeah, yeah, I know it's not a reasonable phobia, but that's kind of the thing about phobias, isn't it? They're not necessarily reasonable. If you have a terror of elevators, it isn't going to evaporate if I produce statistics showing how remote the chances are that you'll plunge to your death if you decided to ride an elevator. Hell, not even if you rode one non-stop, all day long for weeks.

Just the same, maybe a word or two from Tammy would

have eased my mind. If she'd have just given me a thumbs up. Or maybe two, one for each… Uh, never mind.

As it happened, Dr. Tammy Drammen didn't say anything. She just looked very, very confused.

"Let me help you get seated," Hugh offered, pulling out the vacant chair between Dylan and Morris.

Dylan gave me a worried look. Yikes. Note to self: never discuss any potential nut sack growth in front of your boyfriend.

I quickly shot him a little no-worries shake of the head—one that only he'd catch.

Damn, why are relationships so hard?

Murmuring a thank you, I took my usual seat—Dylan on my right, Morris on my left, and Mrs. Presley on the other side of Dylan. Hugh walked around to the head of the table. As I edged my chair a little closer to the table, my toes hit something furry. Humphrey, I realized. Thank God the contact had been fairly gentle. Nevertheless, it was enough to persuade Humphey to relocate. With a groan, the old dog stood, squeezed his way out between me and Dylan, and padded stiffly to Hugh's side. His tail was already wagging in expectation of the petting he was about to get. Hugh didn't let him down.

"There's a good dog, Humphrey."

Humphrey sat, his tail thump-thumping on the floor. Dinner about to be served or not, it didn't look as though he was going anywhere.

Directly across from me were Tammy and Allen. Elizabeth had settled into what had to be the former/late Mrs. Drammen's chair.

"I think we could use more wine." To emphasize her point, Tammy tipped the second glass back, finishing it off.

"I'll get it," Caryn said.

"Sit, dear," Hugh said. There was one empty chair left at the table, and it was meant for her.

"Well, I thought with Elizabeth's mother and grandmother

here, you might like me to help with the meal."

"No need," Hugh said. "Glori and Lois can handle things."

"If there's help needed out there," Mrs. P offered. "I certainly know my way around a kitchen."

Hugh chuckled. "Don't I know it, Nanny Jane. Those pumpkin pancakes were delicious."

"Oh," Caryn started. "Not the usual danish, sausage, and bacon?"

"Sometimes a change is good for the soul," he said.

"Amen to that," came a voice from the doorway.

"Roma!" Tammy was clearly delighted to see her daughter. She leaned back in her chair as Roma came around for a hug. The girl then scooted to give her grandfather a hug.

"When did you get in?" Tammy asked.

"Just now," she lied.

Roma cast Dylan, then me, a quick and meaningful glance. One that said *You tell, and I tell.*

"Roma, we have guests," Elizabeth said. She made the quick introductions of Nanny Jane, me, and Magnus.

"Hey, Dad," Roma said. She didn't close in for a hug.

"Roma." Allen nodded. "Lucky for you to catch a ride in such a bad storm."

"Yeah, wasn't it? My friend's returning to Toronto Monday morning. Maybe afternoon. Um, we might even head back Tuesday."

Roma picked up a chair from beside the enormous sideboard and carried it to the table. She squeezed it in beside her mother. Tammy put an arm around her for another quick hug.

"Why aren't you at school?" Allen asked.

She shrugged. "My friend was coming down for the weekend, so I thought I'd come home for, you know, dinner. It's been a couple weeks."

"School going well?" Hugh inquired, dryly.

As if he didn't know!

"Um, sure, Gramps."

"I'm so glad you came home," Tammy said. "What a lovely surprise."

"I missed you guys." Roma aimed a smile at Caryn. "And I've been so looking forward to one of Caryn's home cooked meals."

She was lying through her teeth. Okay, maybe not about the meal. But the rest of it? She was slinging pure bull.

"You're in for a treat," Elizabeth said. "Glori and Lois made Caryn's yummy duck with orange sauce."

"And it's ready," Glori appeared in the doorway. "Though I don't imagine it'll be as good as Caryn's."

"I'm sure it'll be great," Hugh said.

"Shall I serve now?"

Elizabeth smiled. "Please."

She scooted back into the kitchen.

"Who made those pumpkin pancakes this morning?" Roma asked. "They were awesome!"

Allen turned to look at his daughter. "I thought you just got in?"

Roma looked suddenly very, very busted. But she wasn't about to give it up. "I came in through the kitchen and snagged a leftover one out of the fridge."

"Leftover?" Mrs. P tilted her head towards me. "The way this one eats, I'm surprised there were any."

"Gee, thanks," I said. "But I did leave a couple." And I had, albeit small ones.

Roma looked at me. And I hoped for a quick thank you nod. But those eyes were narrowed in more of a keep-it-up command.

The door from the kitchen swung open, and Lois and Glori began carrying in platters and bowls of food, each dish looking more succulent and delicious than the last. As Lois placed the last dish, Glori produced a bottle of Kooyong Pinot Noir from the sideboard. Honestly, the sight of it was even more mouth-watering than the food.

"This is the right stuff, Mr. Drammen?"

I could hear a note of anxiousness in Glori's voice. Since the bottle had obviously been pre-opened to breathe, I figured Hugh would tell her it was exactly right even if it was a Sauvignon Blanc. But Tammy, possibly the only one in the room more anxious to sample that wine than me, beat him to it.

"Looks good to me," she said.

Hugh studied the label and nodded.

Glori hesitated, clearly a little lost. Hugh smiled at her patiently, tilted his head toward his glass.

"Oh, sorry. I forgot that bit." She poured a small amount into his glass.

He swirled the wine, sniffed it, and then sampled it. "That's fine, Glori." He nodded to her to pour. "It's your first real dinner party with company. Hard to remember everything."

Glori gave him a grateful smile and began moving around the table, pouring the wine carefully for each of us, pausing only to trade the empty bottle for a second one of the same vintage. When she skipped Caryn, no one gave it a second glance. Except me. And when I looked back at Caryn, her eyes were locked on mine.

"You do that a lot," she said.

I blinked. "What?"

"Watch people."

"Oh, do I? Bad habit, I guess."

"Maybe it's a family trait?"

My head shot back.

She smiled. "Your mother's pretty observant too. She worked around our kitchen as if she owned the place."

"Good eyes," Mrs. Presley said. "Well developed from hours of bingo."

The pins and needles tingled all the way up my spine. That wasn't what Caryn had meant. At all.

While the wine had gone around, Lois had served up the duck. Oh my God! My mouth was literally watering.

"Bon appetite," Hugh said.

"This looks delicious." Dylan tucked right in.

It *was* delicious. I'd had duck before but never like this. It was melt-in-your-mouth tender, and the orange sauce was out of this world. The wild rice and asparagus were damned near perfect. If there was cheesecake coming for dessert, I'd be having an orgasm right there at the table.

Ah, the memories…

"Did you make this duck, Glori?" Tammy asked. "It's really good."

Glori was on her way back in from the kitchen, thankfully with another basket of that yummy rosemary bread. She blushed as she answered. "It's Caryn's recipe. She kind of helped."

Caryn shook her head. "Don't sell yourself short. You did all the work."

Allen speared another tender morsel. "Caryn never made anything this good."

"You're wrong there, Allen," Morris said.

"So, Nanny Jane." Hugh raised his voice to shut down Allen and Morris before they really got started. "I hope you had an enjoyable day?"

Mrs. P didn't miss a beat. Though it was kind of weird hearing older-than-dirt Hugh Drammen calling her *Nanny*. "We did. A great day. And tonight, Tammy and I are going to play TV bingo on the big screen."

Tammy's fork clanged to her plate. "What? Bingo? Me? I don't think so, Nanny Jane."

"Just come keep me company, then. It's only about a half hour long."

What the hell was up with Mrs. Presley? She seemed awfully anxious to have Tammy's company for bingo tonight. Was she trying to punish Tammy for her incivility the night we arrived?

"I really don't think so," Tammy said.

Apparently, Mrs. Presley wasn't inclined to take no for an

answer. "Oh, come on, humor an old lady. I never get to play bingo on a giant TV like yours. And besides, you bought way too many cards. I'm pretty sure I didn't ask for so many."

Hmm, I was pretty sure she did.

"Okay, you win," Tammy conceded. "I'll join you and keep you company while—"

Hugh's hand crashed down on the table so violently that everyone gasped.

"Hugh!" Elizabeth cried.

Humphrey started barking wildly—desperately—for someone to do something.

Everyone's eyes were on Hugh. His face was turning redder by the second.

"Oh no!" A stricken Caryn jumped up from the table and raced into the kitchen.

"His EpiPen," Tammy commanded. "Allen, get it now!"

"Hurry!" Elizabeth shouted.

Allen was on his feet in seconds, pulling open the top drawer of that sideboard so hard and fast that it hit the floor. And out flew its contents. Allen fell to his knees and frantically started sorting through. "I can't find it," he said.

Dylan leapt up, but Tammy got to Hugh first.

"Allergic reaction?" Dylan asked.

"Yes," Tammy said grimly. "Help me lay him on the floor."

Tammy might have been on her third glass of wine, but there was no sign of impairment of any kind as she examined her father with sure, steady hands.

"It's not here!" Allen roared. "The pen is gone!"

"Roma, get my bag from my room. There's adrenaline in there."

Roma tore out of the room.

It finally struck me—I had an EpiPen in my purse. The purse that was never far from reach. I grabbed my bag from the floor, rooted through it, and came up with the precious injector.

The door between the kitchen and dining room swung open, smashing against the wall guard hard as Caryn rushed in. "I've got—"

"Here! Use mine!" I held it aloft.

Tammy grabbed it from me and brought it down hard on her father's pants-clad thigh. Having read how those things worked, I knew the auto-injector was designed to stab right through clothing. Every second counted when it came to anaphylactic shock.

Hugh's breathing improved immediately. Roma arrived just then with Tammy's bag. "Is he going to be okay?" she asked, her tone desperate. "Please, Mom, tell me—"

"He's going to be fine, sweetie." Tammy took her medical bag from Roma. "D had an EpiPen on her, thank God."

Tammy took something else out of her bag and administered it to her dad and then started taking his vitals.

"Anything I can do?" Dylan asked.

She sent him a grateful glance. "No, I've got this. Just give him some room and some air."

Dylan came to stand beside me.

"D?" He looked at me like I was a stranger. "You carry an EpiPen?"

"Of course. My tofu allergy."

"I thought that was just an aversion," Mrs. Presley said.

Why does everyone think that? Do they seriously think I'd fake an allergy just because I didn't want to eat something? Just so that if someone presented me with that disgusting bean curd dish, I could whip out my EpiPen and call *allergy* to get out of eating it?

Brilliant, I know. It was bound to work for all things rhubarb too.

"Well, I do seem to have made a spectacle of myself, haven't I?"

That from Hugh, who was now sitting up on the floor.

"Not at all, Hugh-Bear." Elizabeth knelt by his side. "I'm just glad Mother had her EpiPen on her."

“So am I,” Hugh said wryly. “I’m thinking that chair looks more comfortable than this hardwood.”

Dylan was there immediately, helping Tammy get the old man up and back onto his chair.

While all eyes were fixed on Hugh, I took the opportunity to scan the room. Morris was holding onto the collar of an agitated, whining Humphrey, while Allen and Roma fluttered around the edge of the action. All of them wore anxious looks. Caryn, Glori, and Lois stood in the doorway. If anything, they looked even more distraught than the family.

I glanced at Mrs. Presley, who’d come to stand with me. The look in her eyes matched what I was feeling.

Shit had just gotten a whole lot more serious.

CHAPTER 16

HUGH DRAMMEN refused to go to the hospital. Or as he put it, "No way in hell am I going anywhere." In response to Tammy's pleas that he get checked out, he'd responded that he'd be perfectly fine because his daughter-the-doctor was right there.

It was a short-lived argument, which told me that they'd had this discussion before. And that Hugh had won before. He'd rest in his study, with his cold Guinness in his Ocktoberfest mug. His plate of seven saltines topped with Edam cheese and seven gherkin pickles, all counted out. And of course, his beloved Humphrey.

Poor Humphrey. He'd been stressed out of his doggie mind. Tail tucked up between his legs, ears pinned back, the old dog had looked completely woebegone.

The only person who looked worse was Glori. She'd been crying non-stop.

Oh, and no one was going to be fired either. Not Lois, to whom the maple syrup belonged—seems she had a pretty severe French toast addiction and she kept her own personal stash. And not Glori, who hadn't even known about Hugh's allergy, but who swore she hadn't added a drop of it to the recipe.

"And didn't you see me, D, putting the syrup back when you were done with it this morning?"

I hadn't.

"I did." I said. "I'm sure of it."

Yes, I lied. Why not? I could tell just by looking at her—the hand-wringing, the brokenness on her face—that Glori hadn't put maple syrup in the dinner.

But someone had. This was no accident.

Now that her father was okay, Tammy allowed herself to be extremely pissed. Roma mumbled something about wondering how sturdy the table was, and Allen...

After the near-crisis, Allen had to sit back down—elbows on table, head in hands. By all appearances, he was as unsteady as Glori and Lois. Caryn stood back from the table, shaking her head in disbelief. Morris had his arm around her, awkwardly offering comfort. Elizabeth? Despite Tammy's presence, she was still checking the vitals. Well, when she wasn't shooting incinerating death rays my way.

And I deserved every damned one of them.

An hour later, Dylan and I waited with Mrs. P in the big screen viewing room. Spectacular? It was awesome. Dark panelled walls. Two rows of theatre-red padded seats. Remote control, adjustable lighting, and a screen that was almost as tall as Dylan.

Speaking of Dylan, he put his arms around me and whispered in my ear. "Are you thinking what I'm thinking, Dix?"

I nodded. "I think so. Porn, right?"

His head shot back. "Football."

A studied him for a moment. "Liar."

He smiled, as he pressed a little more hip into that hug. Yeah, I was thinking it wasn't football that was giving rise to that promising semi…

Semi? Oh, surely I could do better than that. I held him closer, and in a breathy voice, I whispered, "Maybe we could make a little movie ourselves. Something...I don't know...animalistic. We could play our own little game of *personal best*. Get out some warm oils, light some candles, maybe we could finally try out those fur-lined hand—"

"You two know I'm here, right?" Mrs. Presley said.

Dylan and I shot apart.

Right. Mrs. Presley.

Bingo wouldn't be for another forty minutes or so, but she wanted to be ready when that first bingo ball dropped. And was she ever: troll dolls on alert, dabbers on standby. And cards assembled on a folding card table that no doubt Morris had set up. Assembled for two, no less.

But bingo wasn't the only reason for her love of that room; I knew better. I knew better because she told me—seriously, sometimes being a PI is just that easy. She wanted to see if she could find wrestling on the giant TV.

Mrs. P found her wrestlers, all greased up. Tammy would be along shortly. But in the meantime...the door banged open.

The heavy door hit the stopper and snapped back against Elizabeth's open palm. She slammed it closed behind her as she blasted into the room.

"Dix Dodd," she yelled. "What the hell is wrong with you?"

What was wrong with me?

Not a damned thing. Hey, I'm a woman over forty; I've beaten what's-wrong-with-me with the goodbye stick, baby. A few times.

Maybe I'm too humble? Wait...nothing wrong with that.

It turned out Elizabeth's question was rhetorical. Before she could tear into me, Mrs. P spoke.

"Well, if it isn't my little Boo-Boo! Come to play bingo?"

Elizabeth had eyes only for me. "Looking for Dix." And those eyes were flaming mad. "I looked all over this freakin' house."

"Oh, did you check our room?" Mrs. Presley asked.

"Of course." Elizabeth spared Mrs. P a puzzled glance. "Why?"

"Did you see Dix's new penis?"

"You've seen one, you've seen them all," Elizabeth replied, unfazed.

That was so not true. But I didn't think she was really looking to discuss that right now.

Mrs. Presley was smiling.

Elizabeth was not. Oh boy, she looked pissed. Maybe she had a right to be. And honestly, despite my afore-attested-to perfection, I'd already started berating myself.

I had been given a job to do. So far, not so good.

Elizabeth had paid me well to do that job. Damned well. And, in our own odd little way, she was my friend, as well as a client. I'd let her down on both counts. I hadn't yet figured out who was trying to harm Hugh. Correction: who was trying to kill him. The stakes had definitely been upped at dinner. That fact hadn't gone unnoticed by Mrs. Bee-Drammen.

Dinner had been pure fiasco. More specifically, it had been my fiasco. Well, near fiasco. But now it was time for something else. Time to cover my own assets.

Fists clenched, Elizabeth looked ready to light right into me. I cut her off.

"Before you say anything else, Elizabeth," I said "Let me say right off the bat—you're welcome."

"I'm welcome? What are you talking about?" Her eyes looked like they would pop right out of her head. "Are you completely nuts?"

"Weren't you going to get that printed up for your business cards, Dix? *Are you completely nuts*?" Dylan said, attempting to inject some levity into the situation.

Mrs. Presley laughed out loud. She was the only one. Then she sat back and watched as I tried to dig myself out from under the shit storm I was in for.

I took a deep breath. "Let me explain."

Elizabeth's chin jutted forward. "Go for it."

"The EpiPen," I said. "Do you think I carry one around just for the fun of it?"

Crack. Already I could see the ice breaking around her, but she still looked skeptical. "I take it you have allergies?"

"No," I said. "Sure, I have aversions. Strong ones. Am I the only one who gets it that tofu is actual *bean curd*? Like...from beans. Blech!"

"Dix, stick with the question."

Fair enough. "Do I have allergies? No. You wanted me to keep your hubby safe. And dammit, Elizabeth, that's what I did."

"You knew Hugh was allergic to maple syrup?" She sounded skeptical.

"I figured some kind of allergy was a possibility. And in the off chance that whoever's trying to harm him took that route, I was going to be ready."

Holy crap! It sounded so good I was starting to believe it myself. "Now you know what separates the good PIs from the great PIs."

"Meds?" Mrs. P offered.

"No." I pointed to my head. "It's up here."

"That unibrow thing you get waxed away every month?"

Jesus H. Christ! The woman just was not helping.

I glanced at Dylan. *Ah, a nut sack and unibrow, just what every boyfriend wants to picture...*

"It's forethought!" I shouted before Mrs. P could offer any more suggestions. I stared at Elizabeth. "I'd heard you asking Starla what was in the smoothies at the Cuddle Club. You wanted every single ingredient. When she told you flavoring, you told her to be more specific."

Elizabeth looked thoughtful. "And from that, you concluded Hugh might have an allergy?"

"Like I said, the good from the great, Elizabeth." I fought the urge to bow humbly. "The good from the great. So when I was preparing for this case, while I was getting everything in order, my mind, my notes, every damned thing a great PI would need, I remembered that conversation. And grabbed my EpiPen."

"Don't you need a prescription for those?" Elizabeth asked.

"I've a friend who's a beekeeper," Dylan said. "He fixed us up a while ago with a couple."

Nice. Quick thinking on Dylan's part. Actually, I did have a prescription for the EpiPen, but to say so would blow my story.

Elizabeth studied me a good two minutes before she sat down and exhaled a long sigh. "Sorry, Dix. Thank you...thank you for saving my husband."

Crap. Now that she said it, I felt kind of guilty. Guilty enough to come clean? Nah. I'd get over it.

Elizabeth looked exhausted now that we were out of confrontation mode. In a very un-Elizabeth-like moment, she looked very small to me. Scared. Even Mrs. P held her tongue as the young bride lowered her head in her hands. "We always keep Hugh's EpiPen in that drawer in the sideboard," she said. "Whoever took it knew damned well what they were doing."

"Who knows about Hugh's allergy?" Dylan asked.

She looked up at him. "Everyone. It's not like a corporate secret or anything."

"Lois?"

"Yes, she's been here for years. And let me tell you, she wouldn't be here another minute if it wasn't for Hugh. He's too damned soft."

I was gonna suggest some pills for that...but I let it go.

"Despite what she said, I'm not sure whether Glori knew about the allergy or not," Elizabeth continued. "We hired her right before Caryn got out of the hospital. Surely it didn't slip Lois's mind to tell her."

"Out of the hospital?" That piqued my interest. "Why was Caryn in the hospital?"

"She hurt her back," Elizabeth said.

"Right. That I got. But no one ever said how she hurt her back."

Elizabeth shrugged. "Is it relevant? Hugh would rather we didn't talk about it."

Reluctance again. But loyalty again. Already, Elizabeth was part of the hush-hush, keep-it-in-the-family mentality. Protect one another; protect Caryn. Whatever the reason, by that reluctance, I knew the answer to my next question.

But I asked it anyway. "How drunk was Caryn on the night she hurt her back?"

Elizabeth hesitated long enough for me to know I'd guessed correctly. Finally, she answered. "Pretty damned drunk. Pissed."

"Been there," Mrs. Presley said.

"Haven't we all?" Dylan put in.

I could certainly attest to that too. There were more than a few times when Rochelle and I had overdone our celebrating. Or lamenting. Or when the ball game went into extra innings. Oh, look, another Friday. And then there was that Stones concert…

"It was a one-off thing," Elizabeth said. "But you're right, Dix. It was a day or two before the wedding. She poured herself the first stiff drink she'd had in years. Actually, a couple of stiff ones. Then she decided to go for a midnight stroll."

"Where?" Dylan asked.

"The trails."

"You mean, around the yard?" I asked.

"Farther. The trails are mostly snow-covered now, but they weren't in November. The stretch beyond the gate connects with the city walking trail. Caryn took a tumble. Luckily, she had her cell phone on her, and she called the house. Allen was home. He went looking for her and found her flat on her back on the icy ground. By the time they got back, Caryn was so sloshed. God, she reeked of booze! Tammy came home a half hour later. Wow, she was upset."

"Upset as in mad?"

Elizabeth leaned back as if exhausted. "Upset as in worried. Caryn's worked for the Drammens forever—since she was in high school. She's part of the family."

"Was that why she wasn't at the wedding?" Dylan asked. "Because of her back?"

Elizabeth nodded.

I had a better question. "Was that the only time Caryn got intoxicated? Just that once when Allen retrieved her?"

"That was just the beginning of it," Elizabeth said. "Poor Caryn—it got worse. She was in a great deal of pain with her back, and because of her problem with substances, Tammy was reluctant to prescribe much in the way of pain killers. Just very low dosage. And so…"

"And so Caryn started medicating herself," I said.

"She did," Elizabeth said. "She spent a week either drunk or passed out. Hugh convinced her to take a stint in rehab. It was really sad."

"Poor thing," Mrs. P said.

"Hugh sent her to a facility in New Jersey," Elizabeth said. "Very private. Very expensive. She came home sober. Incredibly remorseful."

"Caryn's back was never the same. It still bothers her. A lot. She's—"

Elizabeth's cell phone rang. Immediately, she stopped talking and dug it out of her pocket.

"It's Hugh," she said, looking at the call display. She sat up straight and put a smile on her face before she answered brightly, "Hi, Hugh-Bear."

I watched that smile fade away. "Okay. I'll tell her. We'll be—" A pause, one that brought a frown to Elizabeth's forehead. "If that's what you want." She ended the call, and looked at me.

"Did your husband just call you from *inside the house*?" I said.

Her lips tightened with the implied criticism. "He's not

lazy, Dix Dodd. And he's perfectly fit enough to come and find me. But he does call sometimes when he wants to save the old dog some steps. Otherwise, Humphrey would tag along after him."

Crap. "Of course. That makes total sense." In an effort to shift the focus from my insensitivity, I said, "What did Hugh want?"

"He wants to see you in his study."

"Now?"

"Right now."

Dylan stood. "Let's go."

"No," Elizabeth said. "He wants to talk to Dix alone."

The door to the viewing room flew open. Elizabeth stood as Tammy entered.

"I was just leaving," Elizabeth said.

As they parted, Tammy and Elizabeth exchanged glances but no words. At least that time those glances weren't filled with animosity. Just a boatload of worry.

"Right on time for bingo," Mrs. Presley announced happily. "And girl talk, naturally."

CHAPTER 17

SO FOR THE second time today, I made my way to Hugh's study. As always, the grandfather clock in the hallway commanded my attention. Everyone was so impressed with that Queen Anne desk, but honestly, I thought the old clock was the most impressive piece of furniture in the mansion. I gave it a closer look. Unmarred, solid maple, and still keeping time perfectly. Well, it agreed with my wrist watch, which read six fifty-five.

I stood there a moment before I pressed on to the study. No, I wasn't nervous or intimidated. Perish the thought. But I was thinking it through.

Why did Hugh want to see me? Now and alone?

Did he want to thank me for saving his life? Was that it? I threw that question out there. Or perhaps more accurately, I threw it *in there*, mentally. Did that *feel* like the answer?

No. Not entirely, anyway.

Hugh Drammen knew I was Dix Dodd, PI, not Elizabeth's mother, D Bee. No doubt he'd made "Magnus" too and would have extrapolated that Nanny Jane was no more Elizabeth's grandmother than he was. Yet he'd allowed us to keep up the ruse for the others. Why? It was a mystery.

Why hadn't I told Elizabeth that Hugh knew? Not so much of a mystery. It was for selfish reasons. No, not just the ginormous amount of money Dylan and I would make on this case. Sometimes it's best to keep details close to the chest. Have I mentioned that I'd been framed before? By a client?

Maybe Hugh wanted my take on things going on around there. Despite what he'd said at the fiasco previously known as dinner, he had to know someone was out to harm him.

Unless...could he really believe it was no more than a series of unfortunate events? No one removed the EpiPen; it just got misplaced. Neither Lois nor Glori had any knowledge of maple syrup being added to the recipe, yet it had obviously made its way into the meal. The fire? Spontaneous combustion! The slip on the mat? He certainly wasn't the first senior citizen to take a tumble.

No. No way. His excuses were bullshit. I knew it. Elizabeth knew it.

And I was pretty sure Hugh knew it too.

Hugh hadn't yet arrived when I let myself into his study. Of course, I was early. I knew he wouldn't keep me waiting long. Instead of sitting, I walked over to the nearest shelf-lined wall and examined the books.

I'm more of a DVD collector myself, but Hugh had some interesting reads on his neatly lined shelves.

Did I say neatly? That was the first time I'd been in Hugh's study alone and I took a closer look at things. Holy crap, those books were perfectly aligned! Perfectly...perfect. Caryn had made a big deal about how particular Hugh was about how books were shelved, but frankly I'd suspected that was more about her asserting a degree of authority over the interlopers who'd intruded on her boss's private space. But damn. Every single book was standing straight in polished wooden shelves that looked like they were built for that very collection. No leaners allowed! Every single spine was pushed in exactly to the edge of the shelf. Completely flush.

And yes, by now I knew they were all rare to very rare to oh-my-fucking-God rare.

I walked over to the wall by Hugh's small bar. Judging by the titles, that section seemed to be on physics. I know diddly squat about physics—or diddly stand; I *do* own a FUD—but I could tell with a glance that these were not your everyday texts. That was an odd looking one at the bottom... I peered closer. *Opticks: Or, A Treatise of the Reflections, Refractions, Inflexions and Colours of Light. Also Two Treatises of the Species and Magnitude of Curvilinear Figures*, by Isaac Newton. And yes, that was *one* book. By Isaac-freakin'-Newton. It looked to be a first edition, too. Thank God I hadn't grabbed that one off the shelf the other day! It had to be worth tens of thousands! More if it was signed…

So was it signed by the author?

I looked around and spotted Humphrey curled up on his dog bed, snoozing away. Huh. Guess Hugh did sometimes phone his bride when he was too tuckered to search her out. Then again, he paid the bills around here. If he wanted to summon people by phone, I guess he'd earned that privilege.

The point was, the coast was clear, at least temporarily. And surely I'd hear Hugh coming down the hallway…

I went for it.

I bent, carefully slid the book off the shelf and straightened to examine it. And watched the flaking, faded pages float to the floor. *Shit!* I squatted to retrieve them, setting the book on the floor. And omigod! Watching the fragile back cover come off as I did.

F-uhhhhhh-uck!

Woof.

Christ on a pogo stick! Now Humphrey was up and at my side. He started sniffing around the pages on floor. Great, dog snot on the book!

"Go on, Humphrey." I pushed him gently out the way. The

old dog sat, cocked his head and looked at me as I frantically worked to get the pages back in. Preferably in order. The brittle, brown pages crumbled under my fingers. Humphrey kept watching, until he turned his head. His wagging tail thumped against the floor as his keen doggie sense kicked in.

Which didn't trump my keen knowing—Hugh was coming down the hall. I heard his approaching footsteps.

I desperately started collecting the pages. *Preferably in order?* Screw that.

Upside down, sideways—oh dear Goddess of library science, forgive me—I folded a couple in half and smacked the back cover on again. I tucked it in close to me quickly, just a split second before Hugh walked into his study.

"Sorry for the delay. I was—"

He stopped short when he saw me there, squatting down, rocking on my heels, trying to look casual as I surveyed the spines.

Thankfully, Hugh didn't walk over to his desk, but to a row of fine books on the far side of the room. I shoved—yes, shoved—that fragile book back into its slot.

Oh, hell, I'd *killed* it.

I shot back up, took a deep breath, and turned to look at Hugh.

This, I was pretty damned sure, was not just a social visit. Hugh was standing facing the left-hand wall, head tilted back as he surveyed a row of burgundy-spined books. I waited, feeling more with every passing moment like the kid sitting outside the principal's office.

Humphrey happily trotted over to Hugh.

"Caryn told me you and Dylan were interested in my books," Hugh finally said.

Well, that confirmed it. He hadn't called him Magnus. He'd made Dylan too.

Hugh turned toward me. "Are you a book lover, Dix?"

Crap! At that moment, I would rather be grilled about why I was posing as Elizabeth's mother than talk about books.

"Well, I'm...I'm certainly not a book killer, if that's what you were thinking."

Hugh blinked.

"I...I mean, yes, I love books."

To prove the point, I blindly picked a book off the shelf closest to the door and looked at it adoringly. *Lord of the Flies* by William Golding. I flipped open the cover. 1954, first edition, and—

"Signed by the author," I said. "Wow."

"Indeed," Hugh said. "That copy's worth close to five thousand dollars now."

I closed the book carefully. Very, very carefully

"I was under the impression fiction wasn't welcome in this collection." I turned to put the book back on the shelf.

"Caryn tell you that?" Hugh asked.

I nodded.

"She probably didn't want you going through them. It's mostly math. But there's some architecture, physics, and yes, a very few fiction titles in here too."

"Mixed right in with the nonfiction?" I wanted to see what he'd say and how he'd say it.

Hugh's eyes widened, and he chuckled. "You got me. No more games, Dix Dodd. You know as well as anyone else under this roof that I have my foibles. Order is one of them. They call it obsessive compulsive disorder. Some people can handle change, some people find it terrifying. I'm somewhere in the middle. Fine on some things, worse on others. It helps me in business, but it can be hard on one's personal life."

"These books?" I said. "They're part of it?"

"Definitely these books."

I appreciated Hugh's honestly, but I was also just plain interested. "What about time?"

He chuckled again. "Like me taking my beer at seven o'clock on the dot? That sort of thing?"

I nodded.

"There's a comfort in schedules, for many with my

condition. Though it causes me some discomfort, I can modify it when the need arises."

Like when you met Elizabeth and one specific need arose. One that hadn't risen to the occasion in some time, I'm guessing.

Whoa, thank God that hadn't come tumbling out of my mouth. That would have been one hell of a faux pas—talking about his arousal.

Note to self: do not say arousal. Whatever you do, DO NOT SAY AROUSAL.

"I'm guessing that's not why we're both here, to talk about your cock."

"Pardon me?"

Argh!

"Needs arising!" I said. "I was thinking about your arousal. I mean your—"

"Word salad."

I hesitated. "What's that?"

"Word salad." Hugh nodded, as though confirming his conclusion. "I'm pretty good at identifying tendencies and such in others. I'm guessing you're prone to word salad. You know, mixing words up under times of stress."

Whoa, he really thought that? I sure hoped so. Otherwise, he'd be thinking I wanted to discuss his private parts.

"Am I right, Dix?"

"Purple hairy boozy chop."

Who was I to nip a misconception in the bud when it completely served my purposes?

"Is there anything I can do to help?"

I shook my head. "I'm garlic. I mean, I'm…" I drew a deep breath. Counted to three. "I'm fine. Yes. Quite fine now." I pushed my words out slowly and deliberately. Not saladed up at all.

We walked to the sofa. The very one that Dylan and I had helped him onto the other evening, after he'd tripped on the rug. We sat.

"Elizabeth doesn't know I remember you and Dylan. She doesn't think I'm very observant when it comes to people. I suppose there's a good reason for that…"

"What's that?" I asked.

"It's because I'm not." He chuckled. "Not with most people anyway. Some faces I remember though. And yours is one of them."

"Why?"

He laughed. "There was a man there."

"At the Cuddle Club?" Crap! I hoped he wasn't going to say we looked alike. I lifted a hand to my upper lip, then dropped it again when I realized what I was doing.

"That's right, the Cuddle Club. I don't remember his face, but I do remember how he was looking at you. You've got quite the admirer, Dix Dodd."

I did? I mean, he couldn't be talking about Dylan. Because as he'd just demonstrated, he knew Dylan's name. So who could he be talking about? Albert had been all hands under the cuddle blanket, but he'd died right there during the cuddle session. Gaetan Gough, the proprietor? He'd looked at me with *something* in his eyes, but it sure hadn't been admiration. More like hatred and loathing.

Who the heck did Hugh mean?

I shook thoughts of that old case away. I had a new case I needed to focus on. One I needed to get back to solving. "Do you know why I'm here?"

He arched a shaggy eyebrow. "Because I asked you to meet me here?"

"No, not in your study. In your *house*, posing as Elizabeth's mother."

"You're here at my wife's request, and I've indulged her because I love her very much. For whatever reason, she seems to feel a sense of security when you're around. She'd never admit it, but I can see it in her. Feel it in her. She's fragile in her own way. And I love Elizabeth enough to continue on with this charade if that security is what she needs."

"I'm here because she thinks you're in danger."

Hugh's eyes locked with mine. "She's wrong."

"No, she's not wrong. We both know it. You're a smart man, Hugh. You have to know by now that someone is out to hurt you."

He raised his hand in a silencing gesture. "No one under this roof means to do me harm. I can guarantee that fact."

"You could have died today!"

"I'm alive and well."

"That fall you took was no accident."

"I beg to differ."

"And that fire—"

Hugh's eyes shifted to the charred shelves beside us.

"That was no accident, Hugh."

He looked back at me again, and when he did, those intelligent eyes were steely. Serious. "The debate is over, Dix," he said. "Tomorrow, I would like you to tell my wife that you've concluded your investigation and that the events of late are just a series of unfortunate coincidences. Return whatever she paid you, and I'll quadruple it. Cash money. You have my word. Then you and Dylan and that sharp lady who you claim to be your mother will leave. I'd ask you to do it tonight, but I wouldn't dream of interrupting Nanny Jane's bingo game. Nor would I ask you to drive back so late at night during a snow storm."

Who was I to argue?

Seriously, I'm asking...who? *I could quadruple my take and be done with this.*

Aaaargh!

Except I couldn't. I was Dix Freakin' Dodd. I've never been one to mince words. But my mind wasn't churning over what to say to convince Hugh that he was wrong, potentially deadly wrong. My mind was churning with something else: why was Hugh arguing with me?

Why was Hugh Drammen, multi-millionaire and family man, arguing with me about his safety? Possibly his very life?

Hugh stood and reached into the pocket of his smoking jacket. He brought out a thick envelope, no doubt stuffed with—oh yeah—at least a quadrupling amount, judging by the thickness of it. He tossed it on the sofa beside me.

"If this isn't enough, let me know. But you work for me now, Dix Dodd. I'm hiring you right out from under my lovely wife. It happens all the time in business. Don't feel bad—it's all for the greater good. So now you follow my direction. And that direction is, case closed. Matter solved. Leave in the morning."

Hugh moved toward the door but stopped beside a particular row of books. He looked at that 1954 author-signed edition of *Lord of the Rings* that I'd purposely left hanging a good inch over the edge of the bookshelf.

He looked at the book as he spoke to me. "I'm a rich man, Dix Dodd. A very rich man. However, in my old age, that means little to me now. But what does mean the world to me is my family. And if there's one thing I know, it's this." With a quick and practiced shove, Hugh slid the book back home. Lined right up with the edge of the shelf. "No one wants to hurt me, Dix."

No one wants to hurt me.

He was telling the truth. And that's when it dawned on me.

On that punctuating line, I knew exactly who had added the maple syrup to the duck, removed the Epi-Pen, took the safety rings off the rug, and most importantly, set the fire in the study.

"Goodnight, Dix."

I answered him with a reflexive goodnight of my own, and he left.

I sat there looking at the thick envelope on the sofa beside me. When Hugh had tossed it down, some bills had fanned out of the unsealed back. Lots and lots of bills. I picked it up. Quadruple? He must have thought Elizabeth had paid me one hell of a lot.

Winter tires for my car? Winter tires for everybody's car!

You work for me now, Dix Dodd. I'm hiring you right out from under my lovely wife.

"Happens all the time in business," I muttered. "Happens all the time."

With the wad of money clutched to my chest, I lay down on the sofa. But I didn't close my eyes for a second. I stared up at the ceiling, stared up at the rows of books above. My mind was churning.

CHAPTER 18

BY MIDNIGHT, IT had stopped snowing, and the sky was that awesome deep-night black and dotted with stars, as it always seemed to be after a heavy snowfall. I saw it because I was outside beneath it. Morris hadn't been around yet to shovel the trails, though I was sure that in his complete efficiency, he'd be on it before dawn. But I found myself standing at the back of the huge home, staring at the brilliant white snow around. It was beautiful. Reflective.

It made me think of lots of things.

Myles Gauthier fell down a well last October. Seriously, the guy took a plunge into a real well, in real life. Not just in my imagination, where he'd fallen down many a well over the years. My ex-fiancé actually emailed to tell me all about it. He'd been visiting a property in New Brunswick that had belonged to his great-grandfather. The old house had been torn down. Lightning had struck the decrepit old barn, and it had burned to the ground three years before. The apple trees were overgrown and untended. And the dried-up well? Right beneath those rotted boards, covered in a half inch of dirt and old leaves.

Myles had been lucky: when he'd fallen, he had been

fortunate enough to snag a few outgrown, flimsy roots to slow his descent. And luckier still, he had his cell phone on him. And service, no less! He was out of there within an hour. The damage? One sprained ankle and a few abrasions. But it could have been worse. It could have been deadly.

So why did out-of-my-life-for-years Myles Gauthier email to tell me all this? Because he thought that I should know, considering what we'd once meant to each other. Even though it had been an email, I could feel the hanging silence on that closing line.

But the real question I was thinking about Myles's call was this: why hadn't I told Dylan that he'd contacted me? Or that I'd emailed Myles back. A couple times.

Or twelve. Ish.

Not counting the rude jokes I flipped.

It's not like there was anything there between us anymore.

Of course, the winter camping trip was also on my mind as I stared up at the stars. Dylan wanted that so badly, and I'd finally made up my mind about what I would do.

And I thought of Hugh. Okay, I thought about the mother-effing wad of money in my inside coat pocket. I hadn't told Dylan about Hugh's offer, either, and that had me feeling like crap. No, I wasn't planning on keeping the money for myself. I would never do that. It's fifty-fifty all the way between Dylan and me. But it honestly didn't feel like a *what should we do* situation, so much as a *what should* I *do* situation.

Wasn't he my partner?

Only I could make up my mind on this. Only I could make up my mind about a lot of things…

I started walking, kicking through the snow-drifted trails back to the house. Inside, I crept past the door to the bedroom I was sharing with Mrs. P and kept right on creeping until I reached Dylan's bedroom. He was asleep. The sound of his breathing, so peaceful and steady, made a strange ache start up in my chest. But then his breathing changed. Possibly because I shed all my clothes, slid in behind him and wrapped an arm around his waist. He rolled over and greeted me with the sweetest kiss.

I lifted my head. "I have a giant wad of money in an envelope in my coat."

"You do?" He said the words against my throat, and I shivered as his beard-stubbled face rasped my tender skin. "Where'd you get it?"

"From Hugh. He gave it to me to switch horses. It's a lot of money, Dylan. Maybe ten times what Elizabeth was paying us."

His mouth stilled. "And what were his conditions?"

"That I stop investigating and tell Elizabeth I found nothing."

He lifted his head. Even in the darkness of the room, I could see the glitter of his eyes. "Can you do that? The Dix I know wouldn't walk away from an unsolved case, especially with someone's safety and security on the line."

The man knew me too well. "I can, because I know who did it, and I know they don't want to hurt Hugh."

He reached over and snapped on the light. "Okay, let's hear it all."

Hugh insisted we all sit down for one meal together. So breakfast it was. He said he hoped it would be a peaceful one.

Good luck with that.

Not surprisingly, breakfast was a less formal affair than the evening meal. No four-fork place settings, no cloth napkins. Mrs. Presley, Dylan, and I were waiting in the dining room. And I had the distinct feeling that the shiny table usually didn't see much breakfast action. Yes, Hugh would forego his usual warmed danish, turkey sausages, and bacon in his office and join Elizabeth's "family" for a lovely time before we departed.

I hadn't seen Elizabeth since last evening, and I had

absolutely no doubt that was Hugh's doing. He had probably whisked his bride away right after our conversation.

Tammy wasn't needed at the hospital that morning, which was a good thing. She and Mrs. Presley had stayed up well past the end of TV bingo, after which Mrs. P introduced her to TV wrestling and Baileys on ice. Tammy seemed lighter. There was a different air about her. She smiled at Mrs. P and me as she joined us at the table. She even spared "Magnus" a friendly hello.

"Hope you all slept well," Tammy said.

"I slept just great," Mrs. P said. "And you, Tams?"

Tams? Yikes! Was Mrs. Presley baiting the woman?

Tammy chuckled. "I slept great too, better than I have in months. Thanks for asking, Nanny J. Nice to have someone care."

Whoa!

No, let's skip *whoa* and head right to *WTF*. Tammy was okay with Tams now. She'd gone from disdain to tolerance to positively sweet in the span of three days? I had the distinct feeling it wasn't just because we were leaving very shortly.

Lois poured the coffee, and I took a sip of mine. Ah. Perfect temperature. Lovely dark roast. I wrapped my hands around the heavy mug and declined the cream and sugar she offered.

Lois looked like hell. She'd obviously not slept well and had probably spent a good part of the night crying. And I was also guessing there wasn't a microscopic drop of maple syrup left in that kitchen.

"And how about you, D?" Allen asked. "How'd you sleep?" Okay, well at least he'd stopped flirting.

"Fantastically." I did not mention my midnight strolling. Allen didn't need that information. "I got laid."

No, he didn't need that either, but what the hell.

"Niiiice," Roma said from the doorway. Still in her PJs, she sauntered into the dining room and took a seat. She looked as if she'd had a late night herself.

"Psst. Pssssssst."

I gave her a who-me look.

Roma smiled. She toyed with the necklace she was wearing. The weird, fuzzy dice necklace. *My* fuzzy dice.

Ah, the *personal best* game continued. Right. Got it. Now I understood. Roma and her boyfriend had had sex in my car the night before. My little car? I nodded my approval—that was a good one.

Once again, Allen had that pasty green thing going for him. Had he had his morning smoke yet? Judging by his agitation, I guessed not. And had Bean Jones retrieved that mysterious picture for him? I couldn't help but smile, because I knew he hadn't.

"Glori and Lois are a little behind this morning," Caryn said as she walked through the door from the kitchen. "But everything should be up shortly. Really, I should be in that kitchen keeping things on track."

Tammy soothed, "Dad wants you to rest your back. We all do. With an injury like yours, a person can't be too careful."

"Well, it appears I am the one who needs to be a bit more careful."

At the sound of Hugh's voice, we all turned to see him enter the dining room. Elizabeth was dressed in another understated-yet-fabulously-expensive-looking casual pant suit. I had my money on Chanel.

Hugh patted Elizabeth's hand before they both sat down.

He was still trying to make light of all the happenings. And it so wasn't working. But I had every confidence those unfortunate events were about to come to an end.

"Sorry things took so long." Lois, followed by a very red-eyed Glori, pushed two food-laden wheeled carts into the room. Oh my God, it all looked so good. Eggs done three different ways. Bacon fried to a perfect crispness. Thin breakfast sausages. Fresh fruit. Scones and perfect-looking toast. Jam, jelly, peanut butter. And not a drop of maple syrup in sight.

After they'd placed the dishes on the table, Lois nodded to Glori, and they both moved to exit the family dining room.

"Would you two mind waiting a moment?" I asked.

Both women stopped and turned.

"There are some things to be discussed," I said. "And this concerns you, as well."

"Is...is this about last night?" Glori's eyes filled with tears all over again.

I nodded.

Hugh spoke up. "No. There's nothing to worry about. And nothing to talk about regarding last night." His voice rang with finality. "In fact, I think D has misspoken. It's all settled."

Except it wasn't all settled.

I was wearing my favorite black vest, a Ralph Lauren reversible job, and the big fat envelope of money was pressing up against my right breast. Yes, it was kind of hot, but that's not the point. There was fifteen large in there. Fifteen thousand dollars, just to keep my mouth shut, which is what Hugh wanted. And I knew why.

Because he knew just as well as I did who was behind those accidents.

So all I had to do was have myself a scone. Pop a few slices bacon on my plate, grab a half dozen little sausages, pile on the scrambled eggs (seems I was hungry), and keep my mouth shut. No problemo, right?

Big fat wad of rent-for-a-year in my pocket? By way of rubbing up against me, the money answered back.

"Why are you swinging your arm across your body, Dix?" Mrs. P asked.

"Oh, sorry."

But I hadn't come here at the bequest of Hugh Drammen but of his wife. My—*cough, cough*—friend, Elizabeth.

When I stood, Dylan's eyes were locked on mine. He smiled, nodding his approval.

"What are you doing?" Hugh asked, but he soon knew. I walked the length of the table and set the envelope of cash down in front of him.

"Hugh?" Elizabeth said. "W-what's this all about?"

I answered for him. "Isablat jatic."

"Oh for God sake, chew your food," Allen said.

Okay, maybe my timing wasn't perfect. I'd snagged a sausage from the buffet as I'd walked the length of the table. I hastily chewed and swallowed the rest of it. No, not the bite—the whole sausage. Let them wait.

I repeated my answer, coherently this time, "It's about justice."

Time to shine. Time to do what Dix Dodd did best. Better than anyone. Time to spill the truth.

This aha moment was mine.

"The fire, the rug slip, the allergy attack. None of it was accidental," I said. "And I know who's responsible for all of it."

Chapter 19

IN MY HEAD, I heard that *dun-dun-dun-dnnnnnnn* refrain. You know, the big, dramatic pounding of the piano keys at the climax of all those old-time radio dramas or British mysteries? Right after the world's sharpest investigator announces she knows who done it? Er, did it. In the PI business—well, in *my* PI business—that's the sweet sound of victory.

That and *ka-ching*.

I closed my eyes to savour it. Just for a quiet second to mentally relish in those deep, victorious notes. Oh there it was again: *dun-dun-dun-dnnnnnnn.*

"Tammy, why is she doing that?" Caryn nodded toward me and looked to Tammy for some sort of explanation.

"Is she on something?" Roma whispered.

"D," Dylan said. "You were doing it out loud again. The whole dun-dun thing."

Crap.

"Word salad," Hugh said with authority. "We need to be patient."

"What's this all about?" Tammy looked to Mrs. P. "Nanny?"

Before Mrs. P could say a word, I drew a breath and began. "Most of you here know me as D Bee. Elizabeth's long-suffering, hard-working, ever-giving—"

"Oh, get on with it," Elizabeth groaned.

"—mother." I nodded. "But in reality, I'm—"

"You're a private investigator." Roma stood and walked over to the buffet, grabbed a plate and began to load it on. "Hired by my new grandmother to see who was trying to hurt Gramps."

What the…? Roma stealing my spotlight?

Roma turned back toward the table. "Isn't that right, Grammy?"

Well, that set Mrs. P chuckling.

Grammy?

By the look on her face, I could tell Elizabeth did *not* like being called Grammy. It probably matched the look on my face—I did not like being upstaged.

"Roma's right," I said. "I am a private investigator. Hired by Gramm—I mean, Elizabeth."

Dylan shot me a you-did-that-on-purpose look. Well, that was a pretty safe bet.

Morris shook his head. "You too, Magnus? Are you a private dick?"

Dylan nodded. "Sorry, dude. And the name's Dylan, not Magnus."

"I showed you my tools. Let you line up my drill bits. You said they were special."

"They are special. Really special. We'll always have that—"

What the hell? The whole scene had all the makings of a really bad musical!

"What are you investigating, Dix Dodd?" Caryn had been holding her water glass tightly but set it down on the table carefully. "Trying to dig up the old bones for some stupid high school reunion?"

"You remember me?"

Her laugh was unsettling. "I remember everyone from high school. You were the one who hated role call so much. Despised when Mr. Mulligan called out your full name. What was it? Dix—"

"Never mind that name!" I said, cutting her off. Not even Dylan knew my full name. And I wanted to keep it that way.

"What's this all about?" Tammy demanded.

"Double or nothing, Dodd!" Hugh said. His eyes shifted around the table. "And I'll add Roma's refunded tuition to sweeten the pie."

"Her what?" Tammy's eyes widened. "How come we're just finding out about this now?"

"I thought I heard someone in the spare bedroom when I was upstairs vacuuming last week. Was that—?" Lois covered her mouth.

Glori bit her lip.

"Caryn, you must have known about this," Allen said.

"Oh, don't you dare blame her again, Allen!" Tammy snapped.

Elizabeth groaned. "Can we stick to the—"

Morris just had to jump in. "So when you said that mine was the biggest belt sander you ever saw—"

"Man, let it go," Dylan said.

And so it went.

I stared at Hugh; Hugh stared at me, victoriously, dammit.

Well played, old man...well played.

Mrs. P was sitting back with an amused look on her face. Allen was hounding his wife about fidelity and marriage, while she was trying to find out from sausage-scarfing Roma what the hell had happened at school. Morris was still listing the shop parts he'd let Dylan touch. Caryn was shaking her head, at me mostly. Lois and Glori were watching the whole scene with wide-eyes. Elizabeth was trying to explain it all to

Hugh.

I wasn't even trying to shout above the din. I did not like this development. I mean, wasn't the attention supposed to be on me? Why's it never about me?

I caught Mrs. P staring my way. In a calm voice, she asked one simple question: "What would a man do in a situation like this, Dix?"

It dawned on me slowly.

I opened my purse and pulled out the FUD. Using it like a gavel, I pounded on the table. The hollow instrument didn't make a loud thump of solid wood but rather a nice snapping/whack whack sound. Maybe that's why they call it whacking…

Never mind.

But the FUD made enough of a noise—not to mention spectacle—to get everyone's attention. Why, they were positively riveted to the sight of me standing there, penis in hand.

"What the hell," Roma said.

Well at least it shut them all up. And everyone had their attention on me once again. Yep, all was right in the world. Dylan stood. I stood. It was show time, baby. For added emphasis, I pounded the FUD in my hand like a mean teacher with a ruler. Hmm, maybe that's why they called it pounding...

Um, never mind again.

I shoved the FUD back in my purse.

"Now that we have your attention again, as I was saying, I'm not Elizabeth's mother. I'm a PI." I looked at Dylan. "We're both private investigators."

"Told you," Roma said.

"Elizabeth hired us," Dylan said. "And before you get upset, Hugh, she wanted to find out who was trying to hurt you. She did it because she loves you. Really loves you. She wants you safe."

Okay, we'll go with that.

"I'm confused," Tammy said. "Who could possibly want to

hurt Daddy?" She stared down the table at her father. "And why were you trying to stop her from telling us."

"I was doing these things myself, that's why." His eyes shifted to me. "I set that fire myself!"

"Hugh?" Elizabeth looked incredulous. "No, I don't believe it. You're lying!"

"He's not really," I said. "Technically, he started the fire. He just didn't mean to. Someone else meant for him to."

Hugh's face hardened.

"If you ask me," Allen said. "If anyone's out to get the old man, it's her." Allen was pointing at Elizabeth. "Hugh always had a soft spot for that type."

"*That type*?" Elizabeth said. "You mean sweet and sophisticated? Is that what you mean, fuckwad?"

Yeah, that was it—sweet and sophisticated.

"Actually, Elizabeth, my money *was* on you for a while," I said. "Even if you didn't get a cent of the Drammen fortune, if anything should happen to your dear husband, you'd get every gift he ever gave you."

"Are you insane?" she said. "Let me remind you, Dix Dodd, I hired you guys."

"It wouldn't have been the first time someone hired us to cover their tracks."

"Or their assets, I'm guessing," Tammy said.

"And that got me thinking, Tammy." I slid a glance her way. "Why so angry at Elizabeth? There's a shitload of money. More than enough to go around for everyone. And you don't seem the greedy sort. At all."

"Money's never been that important to me." Tammy lifted her head with dignity. "I've always had more than enough. Always will."

"But it was really a love/hate between you and Elizabeth, centered around the Queen Anne desk. Hugh promised it to Elizabeth, but you wanted it more than anything. Why?"

Tammy didn't answer. She sat with her lips firmly pressed together, the color rising in her cheeks.

"Morris showed me the desk," Dylan said. "He's brilliant with this stuff."

Morris shifted with Dylan's compliment. "He showed me all the work he'd done on it. And every single hidden drawer, false bottom—we practically took it apart." Dylan looked at Tammy. "There are no pictures in there."

Tammy swallowed hard. "You...you know about the picture?"

"What picture?" Hugh asked.

"The one Allen told your daughter that he had," I told Hugh. "The one he was blackmailing her with."

"Tammy, you wanted that Queen Anne desk because you thought there was a picture hidden in it," I said. "I heard Allen talking on the phone to Bean Jones, a PI. Not as good a PI as me and Dylan, but to be fair, we were already taken. Anyway, I heard him demanding that Bean *get that picture*. At first I thought it was a compromising picture of Allen himself that he was trying to get back. That he was having an affair."

Dylan and I exchanged a glance, and he gave me an almost imperceptible nod.

We hated to do this—reveal Tammy's secret—but sometimes bridges have to be crossed and sometimes they must be burned down.

"But then it hit me," I continued. "Why the hell do you put up with Allen's assholishness, Tammy? He had to have something over you or on you."

I looked at a sneering Allen and then to teary-eyed Tammy.

Mrs. P nodded to Tammy and smiled encouragingly.

Tammy took a deep, deep breath. "Roma, darling, there's something I have to tell you. I...I'm having an affair."

"Yeah, I know." Roma shoved a buttered toast wedge in her mouth.

"You know?" Tammy eyes widened. "How could you possibly know?"

I took advantage of Roma's full-mouth pause.

"I'll take that question." I paced three steps and then turned sharply back around to the audience, er, I mean, group. "Roma knows things the same way I know things. She's like me in a lot of ways. Yes, young, vibrant, full of life...lover of high fashion socks."

Mrs. P snorted a laugh into her orange juice.

"But our connection goes farther," I said. "Roma is very intuitive, like me. She knows things, with a niggle and a nudge and—"

"And I heard you on the phone with Dr. Crotty, Mom," Roma said. "It didn't sound very professional. Although it *was* an anatomical discussion of sorts. But when I looked up 'yummy bits' in Grey's, it wasn't there."

Dr. Crotty? Dr. Lincoln Crotty, the cardiologist? Oh boy, now that was a familiar name!

Allen looked like he was going to explode, though I didn't believe for a second that any of it was news to him.

"Your father told me he had a picture," Tammy told Roma. "He…he told me he'd show it to you if I ever made him leave. And I was going to do just that—right before he…he found out about Lincoln and me. Now that you're in school, older, it was time. But he said he had a very graphic picture of Lincoln and me, that he'd hidden it in my mother's old desk. I…I guessed it was from one of the times Lincoln and I were together at the hospital. Maybe that time in the empty OR…"

Roma stopped chewing. She looked at her mother with renewed admiration.

"There's no picture," Dylan said. I nodded my approval. Word for word, I'd told him what Allen had said to Bean Jones on that call, and Dylan repeated it now. "'*Tammy's starting to suspect I'm lying... No more excuses. I know what I'm talking about! Get that picture!*' That's what Allen said. Not *find* that picture, but *get that picture.* A picture that doesn't exist yet. Allen was hoping Bean would take one."

"So that's why you wanted the desk," Elizabeth said, softly. "Not just because you hated me."

"Hate you? Elizabeth, I'm thrilled that you make Daddy so

happy. But…I couldn't let that picture fall into anyone's hands!"

"So now you know," Allen sneered. "Now you all know. Tammy's the cheater. The bad guy. The—"

"What I know, Allen," Hugh said. "Is that you've been blackmailing my daughter."

Elizabeth put a hand on her husband's arm. It was kind of a stay-calm move. But it was Allen who was looking rather like he might have a stroke on the spot.

"She cheated on me," Allen said. "With a heart surgeon. She hurt me, and I wanted to hurt her back!"

"She's my daughter," Hugh said. "I don't give a rat's ass if she cheated with the whole blasted surgical staff!"

Roma drew an excited breath. "Did you?"

"Er, sorry, no," Tammy said.

"How far did you go, Allen?" Elizabeth asked. "To hurt Tammy?"

"What are you talking about?" he asked.

"Would hurting my husband, Tammy's father, fall under that hurt-her-back umbrella?" Elizabeth looked ready to kill.

"Don't be ridiculous."

I shrugged. "Ridiculous? You've already stated a motive—vengeance. You had the means."

"The means?" Caryn asked.

"He keeps matches on the premises, along with his cigarettes."

"Matches aren't exactly a prohibited item, Dix. Anyone can buy them."

Yes, he had me on that point. So I said, "Oh, and he smokes in the house sometimes too. A big no-no, huh."

"Dad?" Roma said. "You…you wouldn't hurt Grampy, would you?"

"Of course I wouldn't!"

"Oh wouldn't you, Allen?" Tammy said. "Nothing you do would surprise me anymore."

Elizabeth sat forward in the seat. "Allen, if you hurt Hugh,

I swear—" She left the rest unsaid, but I had a pretty good idea what she was thinking. That same thing I was thinking—how lovely it would be to surgically remove his dick.

"But that match didn't light itself. It needed an abrasive." I turned to Roma. "No one even knew you were in the house when the fire started. You'd been hiding here for what, two weeks?"

"Closer to three," Caryn said. She looked at Tammy and Hugh. "Sorry, Roma made me promise not to tell. I…I didn't want her to leave and have no place to go, so I…kept her secret. She swore she'd tell you soon."

"That's all right, Caryn," Hugh said. "Roma's the one who's not been forthright here."

"You left university to pursue your real love," Dylan said. "Aesthetics. I saw all that gear in your bag—the polishes, the tools."

Actually, both Dylan and I knew why she'd really left university—it probably had something to do with conference room tables, library ladies who knew nothing about love, and campus security.

She shrugged. "So?"

"You had a nail file in among your gear," he said.

Roma looked at Dylan and then me blankly. "So I had a nail file. Big deal."

"And someone used a file to start the fire in the study," Dylan answered.

"*Dun-dun-dun-dnnnnnnn*!" I said loudly. Okay, a couple times, to get everyone's attention.

"Dix, you've got to stop doing that," Mrs. P said, shaking her head.

"A file?" Hugh asked, confused. "I don't understand. I was clearly alone when that fire started."

"Someone wedged a match inside an old book, about an inch from the spine—a threadbare and well-worn spine." All eyes were on me now. "They glued a piece of file onto the shelf and frayed or tore away the bottoms of the pages of that frail, old book. Then they left that book protruding from the others on the shelf, knowing that when Hugh lay down after his Guinness, he would look up, see it jutting out of place, and—"

"Grampy's OCD!" Roma said. "He would have slid the book back into place before he nodded off. He couldn't have helped himself."

"Exactly. And when the match head travelled over the file, it ignited. The hollowing out of the bottom of the book would have permitted the necessary oxygen to get in."

"Makes sense," Roma said. "But just because there was a file doesn't mean it was me who put it there."

"Or me," Morris spoke up. "I know what you're all thinking. It was probably me—the newcomer here. I've got a dozen files in the workshop."

"All nice ones," Dylan said.

"Oh, don't pretend like you care."

Wow, this was getting too weird even for me.

"It wasn't you, Morris," I said. "Nor you, Roma."

"I'd never hurt Grampy," Roma said.

"No, you wouldn't." I looked around the room. "But that's just it. No one was trying to hurt him. I was trying all along to figure out who had something to gain if anything happened to Hugh. But then I realized I shouldn't be looking for who had the most to gain here, but who had the most to lose." And then I said the words I absolutely did not want to.

"Caryn, that's you."

CHAPTER 20

I SURVEYED MY HANDIWORK.

It was like everything else had been forgotten with those words I'd spoken. Tammy's affair, Allen's blackmail, and Roma dropping out of school. All had been revealed because of me.

Come to think of it, I really don't get invited to a lot of parties.

In all my years of being a private investigator, there were very few times when I regretted having ferreted out the truth. But this was one of them.

In that flash as I said Caryn's name, it was like we'd gone back in time to high school, and she was again that painfully anxious kid. Lois sat down in the chair at the door. It was either that or fall down into it, by the looks of her. Glori held herself very tightly. Nope, she didn't know what to do either. Mrs. P didn't register shock. But well, she was Mrs. Jane Presley, a woman well beyond shock. But as Caryn lowered her defeated head into her hands, it was Hugh I stared at.

The man was on fire. No, not literally. There was no one on the premises with pyrokinetic powers. Not even *I* have that kind of mind control. But Hugh blazed those angry eyes toward me.

"You were told to let this go, Dix Dodd," he said, his voice cold.

Right.

"I never was very good at doing what I'm told, Hugh," I said.

Okay, maybe once, when *Fifty Shades* first came out…

"I can't believe it," Tammy said. "Caryn?"

Caryn raised her head but wouldn't meet Tammy's eyes. "I...I'm sorry."

"It really wasn't supposed to go this far, was it Caryn?" Dylan's words were sympathetic, and no, it wasn't one bit of a ploy. "You were never trying to hurt Hugh. Were you?"

She shook her head.

"In fact, you were just outside the patio door when the book ignited," I said. "You knew Hugh would push it in and that within seconds, a small fire would start. Humphrey? He's scared to death of fire, so you spared him the discomfort by putting something in the snack plate."

"Benadryl," she whimpered. "I put it in the cheese. I knew he'd gobble it down and it would make him really drowsy."

"Good thing Humphrey isn't a cat," Mrs. P said. "They're a bitch to pill."

I continued. "You were ready to rush back in to put the fire out the moment it started. Except Morris got there first."

"By seconds," Caryn murmured.

"And the slip on the rug?" Elizabeth asked.

Dylan took that one. "There was one rug on that hardwood floor that was slippable. And knowing Hugh's penchant for sameness, I'm betting Caryn knew the exact path he'd take to the couch."

"You wanted Hugh to fall?" Elizabeth asked. There was that deadly look again.

"N-no," Caryn stuttered. "I wanted to catch him."

"And I'm betting you would have been the one to catch him," Mrs. P said. "If we hadn't rung at the gate."

"Hey, that's right," Elizabeth said slowly. "I was standing there with the beer and tray, and Caryn stopped by the study to… Why *did* you stop by the study?"

She shrugged. "I made some excuse. I wanted to be there so I could catch Hugh when he slipped."

"Just like you also wanted to be the one who put out the fire and the one who was first on the scene with an extra EpiPen to save his life after you put the maple syrup in the duck dish."

"Why?" Tammy asked, her voice soft. "Why would you do this? Caryn, you're like a little sister to me. And Dad's been like a father to you. You told me that yourself, many times. You're loved here!"

"But I'm not *needed* here anymore! Elizabeth looks after Hugh. With my back, I can't even spend much time on my feet anymore, let alone manage the kitchen the way I used to. I...I feel so useless. How long before I'm...I'm of no use at all?"

"How could you even think we'd turn our backs on you because of your injury?" Roma said.

When Caryn's gaze shot across the table to Allen, everything tumbled into place.

Ah, that was how…

"What did you say to her, Allen?" I asked.

I wanted to throttle the little twerp. But I'd have to get in line. Right behind Morris, it seemed. He'd jumped from his own chair, pulled Allen out of his seat, and body slammed him to the wall.

Dylan pulled them apart. Nice and slow like.

"You rat bastard," Hugh shouted. "What did you do to her? What did you say to Caryn?"

"Nothing!" Allen wiped the back of his hand across his bleeding lip. Looked like Morris got one good jab in. Good.

Hugh looked at Caryn. "You've never lied to me—what did he say?"

"When you told me you were getting married, I...I was scared your new wife wouldn't like me and would maybe even kick me out."

"I'd never do that!" Elizabeth said.

"And I'd never marry anyone who'd suggest it," Hugh said.

Neither Elizabeth nor Hugh blinked. Yes, they'd had this discussion before.

Caryn shook her head. "That night when you two announced your plans to marry, I had a couple drinks. But just two. Then I realized I...I was being selfish. Silly. And I was heading down a road I did not want to ever travel again. I poured my last drink right out, but I had to get out of there—away from the liquor cabinet—till the craving was gone. So I decided to go for a walk. I slipped and hurt my back. Then I called home and—"

"And Allen went after you," Tammy said.

"He told me how I...I was an embarrassment to this family and that soon I'd be out the door. He...he had whiskey with him."

"I didn't know she'd drink so much!" Allen said.

I snapped, "All you knew, Allen, was that if you got Caryn drunk enough, she'd tell you who your wife was having an affair with. You needed a name for your fake blackmail to work."

"I was going to tell you everything, Tammy," Caryn said. "I...I was just so ashamed. Allen started telling me how useless I was around here. That I was just a charity case now, like I'd always been." She started to cry real tears. "And that I was a bum under this roof. A drain on resources. And he said none of you would ever want me around after you knew I'd spilled the beans about Dr. Crotty and you. And now that I'm so useless..."

"Oh, you poor thing." Tammy got up from her chair and

went to Caryn. She put her arms around her. "I'm so sorry you've had to go through all this. This is your home."

"Forever," Hugh said.

And that was when a very cool thing happened. First Roma, then Hugh, then Elizabeth went over and joined in the group hug. Even Morris joined, some of his awkwardness abating as he joined his family.

I sat down. "Guess you were right, Mrs. Presley. About family."

"When are you going to learn I'm always right, Dix?"

"You pretty much are."

I caught Dylan's eye. *Well done, partner.* He nodded.

I smiled. We all did. Even Glori and Lois, who were tiptoeing back into the kitchen, hopefully to put on more coffee. Mine was cold. Even Humphrey was wagging his tail as he nuzzled into the group.

Hugh Drammen looked over his group of love to me. "Well done, Dix Dodd."

I pointed at the enticing thick envelope of money, smiling in a hopeful way. An encouraging way.

"Not a chance."

Damn.

"Well that's that," Allen said. "All's well that ends well."

That was when the second cool thing happened. Hugh straightened. He looked at Allen and uttered the words that only such a loving, kind benevolent man like Hugh Drammen could utter in a situation like this.

"Get the fuck out, Allen."

EPILOGUE

IN CASE YOU'RE wondering, Dylan did tell me about Saffron—how they'd dated for a few months during law school and broken up to become really good friends. That was it. I appreciated him telling me.

Oh, and in case you're wondering, I didn't tell Dylan about the emails Myles and I exchanged. I mean, they're just emails.

Right?

We were sitting by the frozen lake.

Dylan reached over and squeezed my knee. I covered his mitten-covered hand with my own a moment before I let it go. The snow was gently falling, the bonfire crackled and threw its cozy heat, and life was pretty darned good.

I had that contended feeling—the warmth of the fire, the boyfriend beside me. Oh yeah, and I was three sheets to the wind.

"Here's to good old times," Chevy said. He and his wife, Colleen, had just gotten back from a skate and rejoined the group, sitting down beside Jack and his husband, Kyle.

Our chalet was the only one rented out that weekend, but the owner still had been kind enough to get the ice shovelled for skating, the bonfire ready for lighting, and the chalet nice and warmed. Oh, and she'd sent over her seventeen-year-old daughter to babysit Saffron's little fellow, Rhett, so we could enjoy our evening by the fire worry free.

Saffron Pratt looked so much like me, she could have been a younger version, which was both flattering and disturbing. We were both blonds, naturally, about the same height. So I didn't mean to...but I liked her right away. Once we got talking, I could really understand what Dylan had seen in her. She was intelligent, had a wicked sense of humor, and was crazy about her little boy.

Despite the sitter, Saffron did venture the long and slippery trek up to the chalet every half hour or so (well, the bathroom was there). She was a single mom to an adorable little boy that looked nothing like Dylan, and yeah, I did make the comparisons. Rhett's father was out of the picture, and they were better off without him, according to Saffron.

I'd yet to make the trek up to pee. Brr, I wasn't looking forward to it.

"Another shot, Dix?" Saffron asked me.

"Sure." I passed over my oversized mug, and she poured me another generous shot of Polar Ice vodka. "Anything to stay warm."

"Amen to that," Chevy said. He twisted the top off another cooler.

Drink in hand, I sat back in the camping chair. Dylan had scooched his chair over, and in a moment his arms were around me. He looked at ease. More at ease and happy than I'd seen him in a long time.

Life's strange. So many folks come in and out of our personal timelines. You might go years without seeing them. But then you do, and it's…well, comfortable. Works out okay. Like Dylan with Saffron, Jack, and Chevy. And me with Caryn Sommers.

Once things had settled down at that most-memorable breakfast, we got some more details. Caryn had worked for the Drammens since she'd left high school. After she left junior year, she got a job at one of Hugh's hotels. Apparently, it was too much for poor Caryn. That sense of security in same time, same place, same people sort of thing. She needed it. Hugh happened to take notice of her, and he helped her out. It turned out that Hugh had left the house to Caryn in his will, as well as a sizable chunk of change. A fact that Tammy had known for years, but Hugh hadn't divulged to anyone else in the family. Caryn was one of them—yeah, family.

And speaking of sense of security, Tammy had spilled her heart to the Baileys-pouring Mrs. Presley. And, not surprisingly, Mrs. P hadn't breathed a word of it to me. But one thing for sure, Allen Boyden was a Class A jerk. Tammy just needed a good dose of Mrs. P's common sense to kick his ass to the curb.

The affair she was having with Lincoln Crotty?

Life happens.

Morris had decided to stay in Ontario for a little while longer. Or a long while longer. If I didn't miss my guess—and I seldom do about these things—he had a thing for Caryn. Everyone was glad to have him stay on. Even Elizabeth. Oh, and that whole misconception about them vouching for each other the night of the fire? Turns out Elizabeth was having Morris look at the grandfather clock. It seemed to be a minute off, and knowing her husband's obsession with time, she had wanted it perfect.

Elizabeth Bee-Drammen was greatly relieved that no one was really trying to harm her Hugh-Bear. I honestly believed she loved her husband. Maybe not as much as her assets...but in her own way.

And Dylan and I were paid in full. By Elizabeth. That fat envelope of cash from Hugh Drammen himself would have been nice. Really nice. But it wasn't to be.

"Hey, remember that time in Professor Heinrich's Corporate Taxation class when you were so hung over, Saff?" Chevy laughed. He leaned over to explain to Colleen. "She'd been seriously into the tequila the night before. Margarita-ville all the way."

"Hey, my twin brother was in town," Saffron protested. "I hadn't seen him in years. What could I do?"

Dylan laughed. "We all were hung over, if I recall correctly."

"Hey, talk about embarrassing," Jack said. "Dylan, remember that time we went to karaoke at the campus bar?"

"Oh yeah," Dylan said. "That was—"

"Awesome!" Saffron said. "You have the most amazing voice."

Oh, dear God! She'd said that with a straight face!

Jack and Chevy exchanged silent glances. Yep, they knew what a horrible singer Dylan was. Their wide grins confirmed it.

"Another shot, Dix?" Saffron had already poured it.

I grabbed the tiny glass and smiled at all of them.

They were happy. We were happy. I liked this, and I felt just like Dylan hoped I would—at ease. His friends were great. I'd taken that leap of faith that Dylan had asked me to, and I was glad I had. Yes, I'd been brave.

And now it was time to be braver still.

I stood.

"Where are you going, Dix?" Dylan asked.

"I have to pee."

He got up. "Let me walk you to the chalet."

"Pfft. Hardly."

The guys had done the walk around the woodshed to relieve themselves. Well, if it was good enough for the guys, it was good enough for pee. I mean for me.

I trampled through the snow around the corner of the building. But barely around. I leaned back and smiled at the fireside group, and I pulled the FUD out from my parka pocket.

I unzipped my pants, pushed them down slightly, and placed the device (thankfully warm, as it had been inside my jacket). I smiled back over my shoulder at Dylan.

This was love, baby. I was peeing standing up!

And when I was done, I shook it like an old pro.

I tracked back through the snow and sat down beside Dylan again.

Aside from the crackling of the fire, there was dead silence.

Finally, Chevy leaned over to Dylan. In a harsh stage whisper, he said, "Um, Dylan, your chick's a dude."

Everyone exploded with uncontrollable laughter, including Dylan.

I opened my mouth to explain I'd been using a FUD, but before I could get a word out, Dylan, turned me into his arms and kissed me silly. "Yes," he said. "And she has the most remarkable breasts."

Chevy frowned. "You mean, for a dude?"

Dylan froze, a look of horror entering his eyes. "No, no, noooo! This can't be happening again!" He turned to the others. "I meant for *anyone*. Man or woman. I mean, she *is* a woman, I swear, despite the dick. I mean, it's not a *real* dick. I should know—I gave it to her."

That produced a whole new round of hooting and laughing.

I could have helped him out, but I didn't. I was already looking forward to reminding him that he was one up in the blunder department. Yes, we really are that competitive.

So as Dylan tried to scrabble his way out of the hole he'd dug for himself, I sat there smiling and said not a word.

Life is weird...sometimes in a very good way.

NOTE FROM THE AUTHOR

Thank you for investing your most valuable commodity—your time—in reading our book. We hope we managed to make you laugh!

Word of mouth is the most powerful promotion any book can receive. If you enjoyed this book, please consider spreading the word. You can do this by:

- recommending it to your friends (literal word of mouth!)
- posting a review wherever you bought it (this is incredibly important, as reviews stimulate the algorithms that make a book more discoverable for other readers)
- reviewing it at Goodreads or other online places where readers gather
- giving it a shout out on social media (#dixdodd)

Again, thank you!

N.L. Wilson
(aka Norah Wilson and Heather Doherty)

Other Books

Dix Dodd Mysteries

The Case of the Flashing Fashion Queen (#1)
Family Jewels (#2)
Death by Cuddle Club (#3)
A Moment on the Lips (a Dix Dodd short story)
Check out Dix Dodd's website: http://www.dixdodd.com

Other books by the writing team of Wilson/Doherty
Young Adult
Ashlyn's Radio
The Summoning (Gatekeepers, #1)
Comes the Night *(Casters, #1)*
Enter the Night *(Casters, #2)*
Embrace the Night *(Casters, #3)*
Forever the Night *(Casters, #4)*—coming soon!
Read about the Casters series at http://castersthebooks.com

Available from Norah Wilson:
Romantic Suspense
Fatal Hearts, Montlake Romance
Every Breath She Takes, Montlake Romance
Guarding Suzannah, *Serve and Protect #1*
Saving Grace, *Serve and Protect #2*
Protecting Paige, *Serve and Protect #3*
Needing Nita, *Serve and Protect - free novella*

Paranormal Romance
The Merzetti Effect—A Vampire Romance, #1
Nightfall—A Vampire Romance, #2

About the Authors

NORAH WILSON is a USA Today bestselling author of romantic suspense and paranormal romance. She lives in Fredericton, New Brunswick, Canada, with her husband, two adult children, beloved Rotti-Shepherd mix Chloe and tuxedo cat Ruckus.

HEATHER DOHERTY fell completely in love with writing while taking creative writing courses with Athabasca University. Motivated by her university success, and a life-long dream of becoming a novelist, she later enrolled in the Humber School for Writers. Her first literary novel was published in 2006. While still writing dark literary (as well as not-so-dark children's lit), she is beyond thrilled to be writing the Dix Dodd cozy mysteries and paranormal/horror with Norah. Heather lives in Fredericton, New Brunswick with her family.

Connect with Norah Online:
Twitter: http://twitter.com/norah_wilson
Facebook: http://www.facebook.com/NorahWilsonWrites
Goodreads: http://www.goodreads.com
/author/show/1361508.Norah_Wilson
Norah's Website: http://www.norahwilsonwrites.com
Email: norahwilsonwrites@gmail.com

Connect with Heather Online:
Facebook: http://www.facebook.com/heather.doherty.5
Email: heatherjaned@hotmail.com